Jesse skidded to a stop, pulling away from Eliza. Squeezing his eyes shut, he spun around in one smooth motion, pulling the gun up to his shoulder and squeezing the trigger. He thought he heard a high-pitched squeal just before the gun's report set his ears ringing.

Jesse risked cracking his eyes open to see if he'd hit anything. The basilisk wasn't far away, rearing back with a bloody scratch along the side of its face. Jesse felt a crushing disappointment. He'd only grazed it. But then a rumbling began under his feet. There was a whoosh of air from the stope opening, and a wave of heat following it.

"Oh, no."

A huge ball of crackling lightning formed and raced toward them.

"Run!" he screamed at his friends. "Run!"

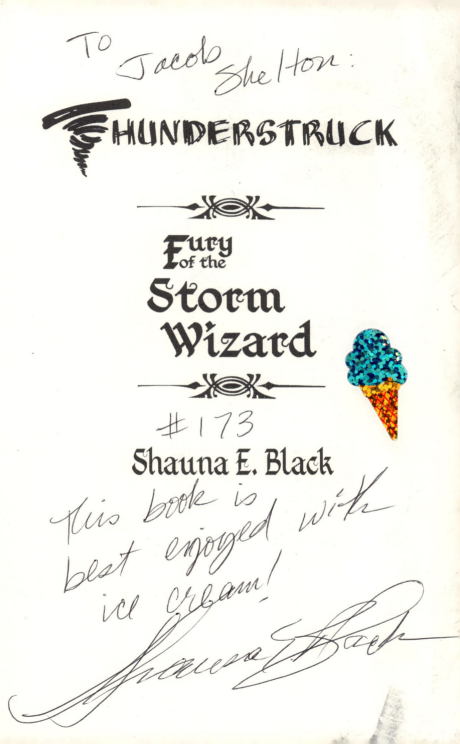

To Jacob Shelton:

THUNDERSTRUCK

—◆◆◆—

Fury of the Storm Wizard

—◆◆◆—

#173

Shauna E. Black

This book is best enjoyed with ice cream!

Shauna E. Black

Fury of the Storm Wizard: a Thunderstruck novel

Text copyright © 2013 Shauna E. Black

Cover illustrations copyright © 2013 Michele Amatrula

Book cover design by Melissa Bigney

Vivienza

Published by Vivienza, Inc.
www.vivienza.com

ISBN 978-1-940855-01-1

Fury of the Storm Wizard / Shauna E. Black

Summary: In Silver Valley, an unusual string of mining accidents has locals whispering of dark magic. When the marshal sent to investigate goes missing, his young assistant Boone turns to Jesse and Eliza for help. But Jesse is a new mage with raw magic, and Eliza is hiding a secret. The three must learn to trust each other before the valley is destroyed and they are ripped away from everything they hold dear.

For Steve

my companion through thick and thin

Contents

Chapter 1
A Cow in Quicksand

Jesse shoved a scrap of yellow gingham into a carpet bag, burying it deep between layers of rough wool trousers and cotton shirts. His room was as hollow as he felt inside, the bed bare of quilt or mattress, the washstand empty.

He fastened the bag's clasp and was about to heft it downstairs when the agitated cackle of a flock of chickens told him a fox was in the henhouse. Jesse's emotions snapped. He dropped the bag, taking the loft stairs two at a time and jumping the last five to snatch Pa's gun from over the mantel.

"Not the gun, Jesse!" Pa's voice held a note of panic as he ran out of the back room.

Jesse's emotions propelled him through the front door and into the yard with the gun already raised to his shoulder. That thieving fox would not get off so clean today.

The fox must have heard Jesse coming. It streaked out of the chicken coop in a blur of red. Jesse took hasty aim and fired.

He missed—and hit the chicken coop.

1

Ice raced up the sides of the coop, covering it with a thick, glittering blanket before Jesse could blink.

Pa skidded to a stop next to Jesse, panting and staring. It was late summer on the Kansas prairie. Ice could not form on the chicken coop any more than a pig could sprout wings. Yet it did.

Jesse felt the ice growing in his gut at the same rate it covered the coop. He didn't say a word, didn't defend himself, didn't protest that it wasn't his fault. Pa wouldn't believe it anyway. Neither did Jesse.

Pa's salt-and-pepper mustache jumped and quivered. Jesse wished Pa would yell, stomp around in a rage, or even whip off his belt to tan Jesse's backside. Pa did none of those things. He turned silently on a boot heel and strode back to the house. Even the door settled quietly against the frame when he passed.

It wasn't the first time this summer that Jesse's intentions had gone awry in a way that couldn't be explained by natural law, especially where guns were concerned. At least the hens would be well preserved when the new owner took possession of the farm. The man's wife would have to be a good cook. They'd be eating chicken and dumplings for a month.

Jesse's thin frame shook inside clothes that were at least a size too big. Pa kept saying he'd grow into them, but Jesse felt like he was drowning. Nothing had gone right since the tornado last May. It was the same day Ma died with a newborn babe in her arms that never drew breath. Since then, Jesse couldn't do anything right. Just over two weeks ago, he was out hanging laundry when a small whirlwind came out of nowhere to scatter long underwear all over the yard. Pa had asked Jesse to quit doing chores for a while. Now the chicken coop was frozen.

Dropping the rifle Pa had brought back from the War Between the States, Jesse turned away from the chicken coop and stumbled to the barn on the far side of the yard.

It still smelled of hay and manure, but the animals were gone, sold last week to pay for the train tickets that would carry Jesse and Pa from Randolph, Kansas, all the way to the Colorado Rocky Mountains. Jesse's older brother, Sam, worked the silver mines there. He said mining offered decent pay. Pa said anything was better than beating his head over and over against this sorry piece of land.

Jesse sagged against the door of Chip's empty stall. The big draft horse had left a dent in the hay where he usually slept. A saddle blanket lay crumpled on the ground, ragged and lost without its owner. Jesse gripped the top of the stall door, ignoring splinters that pressed into his skin from the old wood. Emotions raged through him—confusion, anger, fear, and loss. He'd gone through more trouble in the last three months than any thirteen-year-old kid should have to endure. But he would not cry. He hadn't cried since Ma died, and he wasn't about to start now.

"Paul!" A voice came from the yard. "Paul Owens!"

Pa's voice soon answered. "Right here, William."

"You know there's ice on your chicken coop?"

"I seen it."

"You all get some kind of weather over here."

Jesse edged toward the barn door, peeking around it. Their neighbor, Mr. Lawson, was just climbing down from a flatbed wagon. Two horses stood in the harness, a roan and a bay.

Pa carried a large chest down the steps of the house. Mr. Lawson leaped forward to help him load it in the wagon.

"The new owner, Mr. Fletcher, might not be too happy the chickens are...gone," Mr. Lawson said.

"If he complains, I'll buy him some new ones."

"You that anxious to be rid of this place?"

Pa slid the trunk farther into the wagon and stretched. His eyes looked more sunken than usual as they scanned the yard and the fields beyond. Jesse ducked his head back into the barn before Pa spotted him.

"I need a new start, William. Jesse needs a new start. There ain't nothing left here for us but pain."

"You know best, Paul."

"I got one more trunk and a couple of carpet bags," Pa said.

"Let me help you with those."

Jesse heard the hollow rattle of boot heels hitting the wood planking of the porch. He dashed out the barn door, veering to his left where a young birch, one of only two trees on their five acres, reached its spindly arms toward the sky.

Under the tree, he skidded to a stop in front of a wooden plank standing upright in the dirt. Jesse dropped to his knees beside the plank and reached out to touch a finger to words carved into the wood:

SARAH OWENS, 1840-1879

BABY OWENS

Pa had said Ma would rest easy in the shade of the birch as it grew. She loved trees and missed the forests of her native home in Tennessee.

Jesse struggled to pull a small jar from his pants pocket. He yanked the cork out, scooped up a handful of dirt from the grave, and poured it into the jar.

"Awful good of you to drive us to the stage stop." Pa's voice preceded him out the door of the house.

Jesse jammed the cork back into the bottle and scrambled to his feet, shoving the bottle into his pocket.

Pa spotted him. "Come along, son. Time's a wasting, and the stage won't wait for us."

"Yes, sir."

"Morning, young Jesse," Mr. Lawson said as he helped Pa load the second trunk into the wagon bed.

"Morning, sir."

"You ready for this adventure?"

Jesse scuffed a toe in the dirt and didn't answer.

Throwing the carpet bags in next to the trunk, Pa lifted his hat to run a hand through his thinning gray hair. "Can't say I'll miss this place."

Jesse's eyes wandered to Ma's grave. He felt like somebody had punched him in the gut. He clenched his jaw and blinked fast to keep the tears from spilling over.

Mr. Lawson climbed up into the driver's seat. Pa followed.

"Coming, Jesse?" Pa asked.

Jesse hesitated. He wondered what would happen if he started to run, run like the wind before a storm. It would be good to feel his legs pumping under him, carrying him away from everyone and everything. The wind whipping past his face would dry any tears.

"Jesse," Pa said more firmly.

Jesse pulled in a long, hard breath. It felt like ice crystals, freezing his lungs on the way in. He climbed into the wagon bed and watched the birch tree as Mr. Lawson clucked to the horses and the wagon rumbled away from a farm lost in haze.

Chapter 2
Cutting Out from the Herd

The shrill cry of a red-tailed hawk echoed in the stillness of the afternoon air. Boone Evans casually tipped back the brim of his tan cowboy hat to uncover his eyes, scanning the horizon. The land here was level and covered in sagebrush. It stretched in front of him to the north and west until it hit a distant bluff some five miles away. Not far to the east, a stand of juniper trees formed a dark smudge.

Boone sat against a low wall made of sandstone rocks and mortar. He examined the shadows of the brush and the trees to his left. Nothing moved. But he could smell something. Licorice, with a hint of apple cider and an undertone of musty staleness. He knew that smell.

Boone raised his voice. "You can come out now, Willard."

"Dadgum, Boone! Can't a guy sneak up on you without that schnozzle of yours ratting him out?"

One of the twisted cedar trees unfolded its limbs and transformed into a lanky young man in his early twenties

8

with a bowler hat and a faded purple vest that contrasted nicely with his chocolate coloring. He sauntered up to Boone.

Boone tipped his hat back further and peered up at Willard. "I reckon your ma never told you to keep your socks clean."

Willard plopped into the dirt next to Boone and took the strip of jerky Boone offered.

"It isn't fair," Willard said. "No matter how good I get at that camouflage spell, you always know I'm there."

"I can't help it if you smell like week-old laundry."

"Next time, I'm going to bathe in vinegar. Then you won't know it's me."

Boone wrinkled his nose. "Better if you don't bathe at all for a month and roll around on the ground every day. Then you'll smell just like dirt."

"Really?"

"'Course, you might find yourself short on friends, if you tried that," Boone said.

"It'd be worth it to catch you off guard," Willard replied.

Boone grinned. "Nobody catches me off guard."

Boone handed Willard the rest of the jerky and climbed to his feet, slinging his canteen over one shoulder and stretching legs grown stiff from hours of sitting. He hitched up the bracers he wore and brushed red dirt off the seat of his trousers. The dirt had gotten smeared into the sleeves of his white shirt. It would take some serious scrubbing to get it out. At least his leather vest remained clean.

Taller than Willard by a good head, Boone was five years younger at sixteen, according to human reckoning. He rubbed at the gingery stubble of his first beard. "It's been right quiet this morning," Boone said. "Nothing but chipmunks and rabbits for miles. Honestly, I don't know why they bother posting a sentry way out here."

Willard chuckled. "You never know what evil rabbit will sneak into the Veiled Canyon and cause destruction."

Boone snorted. "Ain't that the truth. See you tomorrow."

"Oh, Boone! I almost forgot." Willard winced. "You were supposed to report to Katsina Vihala a half hour ago."

Boone blinked. "Vihala?" Vihala was the leader of the Katsina, who ruled the Veiled Canyon and supervised the use of magic in the West. Boone wanted to shake Willard until his teeth rattled. "How could you forget about that?"

Willard reddened. "Hey, don't shoot the messenger."

"I ain't getting in trouble for being late. I'm flying."

"You know how touchy the Katsina are about you flying outside the Veiled Canyon."

"Humans never look up. Not until it's too late, anyhow. Besides, I'll get to the boundaries in no time. Then it won't matter if I'm flying."

With a thought, Boone changed form. His surroundings seemed to shrink. Willard became as small as a child as Boone's body expanded. Double horns thrust up through the hidden holes in his hat. Human hair became ginger-colored fur, sprouting around a long muzzle on top of his head and down his back. Scales erupted all over his body, a deep red sprinkled with orange and yellow specks. Smells were sharper—sagebrush and iron in the dirt, small rodents, and a faint hint of moisture from scattered clouds in the sky. Boone whipped his tail to catch his balance as he completed the change into his dragon form.

"Just watch out for Tom Finley," Willard said. "He's on duty at the next checkpoint."

Boone groaned. Tom Finley was the biggest tattletale in the Veiled Canyon. "Thanks, Willard. Be seeing you." Spreading his massive wings, Boone pushed off from the ground.

It was five miles to the Veiled Canyon as the crow flies—or rather, the dragon. Boone took an alternative route so he wouldn't have to fly over sentry points, especially

Tom Finley's. Following a dry creek bed and vast slabs of slickrock on the ground below, Boone made good time.

A shudder went through him as he passed the invisible dome over the Veiled Canyon that kept it hidden from the rest of the world. His worries about someone spotting him sloughed away into relief now that he would no longer get in trouble for flying.

The Veiled Canyon stretched out below him, a crescent gouge in the surface of the earth a thousand feet deep. Boone could just make out movement in the fields of the canyon floor. Although he couldn't discern detail from the air, he knew workers tended corn, squash, and other crops down there. He had been assigned to help in those fields often enough.

There were several cliff dwellings built in caves along the walls of the canyon. Boone angled the path of his flight and headed for the largest, halfway up one of the canyon walls. Filled with tall buildings made from chunky sandstone rocks and cedar poles, the cave was higher than a ponderosa pine and wider than the Colorado River.

Nobody made a fuss as Boone came winging into the cliff dwelling. Although he was the only dragon in the Veiled Canyon, he had lived here most of his life, and the people were used to him.

He shifted back into human form and strode rapidly toward several guards dressed in buckskin and feathers who stood in a circle around a kiva opening near the front of the dwelling. One of the guards lowered his spear to intercept Boone as he approached.

"I'm supposed to report to Katsina Vihala," Boone protested when the guard grabbed his arm.

"Not in there," the guard said. "Come with me."

Boone frantically reviewed his latest escapades with Willard as the guard dragged him at a brisk pace through the warren of cliff dwellings. Just how much trouble was he in this time?

The cliff dwellings were built in layers, each a step higher than the last. It got darker as they moved deeper into the cave, with fewer and fewer people around until finally they were alone next to a small storeroom built against the rear wall of the cave. There were no footprints in the sand around it.

The guard pushed Boone toward the door. "Go in there," the guard growled.

Boone went in alone, wondering if this was some new form of punishment. He had to bend nearly in half to get through the opening. Inside, the floor was covered with dry corncobs and smelled like rat droppings. Boone brought his arm up to his face and breathed through the fabric of his shirt to dilute the stench.

A sudden breeze lifted the hair on his neck. It picked up the dust at his feet, swirling it higher until it reached the ceiling. Boone was able to straighten up as the ceiling lifted and a rough wooden ladder appeared, leading to a square opening that hadn't been there before. Boone hesitated before mounting the ladder.

The opening gave way to a room no larger than twenty paces across and ten deep. It was furnished simply, with woven rugs and animal furs. Smoke trickled from a fire in a stone grate near the outer wall between matching windows.

He glanced out one of the windows and saw the structures of the cliff dwelling. Boone realized this room was built on a ledge he'd never seen from below. There must have been a spell on it to deflect prying eyes.

Three other people were in the room, making it feel crowded as Boone entered. A tall woman with a strong jaw and slanted eyes stood near the top of the ladder. She wore a feathered headpiece and a simple doeskin dress that fell to her ankles. When he saw her, Boone nearly swallowed his tongue. He yanked the hat off his head and sketched a hasty bow. Vihala led the Katsina and made all their decisions final. She was not one to cross or keep waiting.

"Good of you to join us, young Evans," she said quietly.

A man limped forward and thrust a leather bag into Boone's arms.

"Katsina Hassún," Boone said, feeling worse than ever in the presence of his strict tutor.

Hassún's right arm was shriveled, hanging useless at his side. A gold armband circled the bicep of his other arm. He had square features with a prominent nose and small eyes out of balance with the rest of his face.

"This is a bad idea, Vihala," Hassún growled, his eyes all but disappearing in a judgmental squint.

The third adult in the room tossed a small pistol at Hassún that he caught awkwardly. "We've delayed long enough already," the stranger said with a voice full of gravel.

He was dressed differently from the other two Katsina, in leather chaps and a greatcoat with a dark hat sitting low on his head. The strap of a harness crossing his chest held a rifle peeking over his shoulder. Although he was a stranger, Boone thought he knew who the man was by reputation alone. Colorow was one of the Katsina who roved the country acting like a marshal, keeping those with magic in line and hidden from the knowledge of those without it.

"You read the glyphs yourself, Hassún," Vihala said. "Do you believe this Storm of the Century was caused by a mistralmage who only controls the wind?"

"Of course not. Neither do I believe Orendos has returned from the dead."

Boone sucked in a sharp breath. "Orendos? The evil mage?" It was nigh two hundred years since Orendos' reign of terror over the West, but the Katsina weren't likely to forget him anytime soon.

"I didn't say that," Colorow growled as he shoved dried beef and stacks of flat corn cakes into a second leather bag.

Hassún gave him a withering stare. "You said a thundermage was after one of the Wité Pot shards."

"I *said* I heard rumors of an unusual amount of mining accidents in the Rocky Mountains, and the weather patterns indicate that a thundermage is moving in that direction."

Vihala frowned. "If there are mining accidents, then our agent Nukpana is likely in need of assistance, whether a thundermage is involved or not."

Orendos and the Wité pot. Boone didn't remember the Katsina ever discussing the dark mage who had imprisoned them. It wasn't exactly a subject for polite conversation. The world was spinning around him. Boone wobbled toward a pile of furs and sank down.

"Not now," Hassún barked, pulling Boone back to his feet. "You're going with me to the travel chamber. You and Colorow are leaving the Veiled Canyon right now."

"W…what?" Boone stammered. "Why?" He hadn't been more than twenty miles outside the Veiled Canyon since his mother had abandoned him when he was a small child.

Hassún's manner was impatient and cross, as if Boone's questions were a personal affront. "Haven't you been listening, Evans? There is a thundermage headed for the Rocky Mountains, where one of the Wité Pot shards is hidden. You must go with Katsina Colorow to investigate."

Colorow picked up a knife from a rock shelf and slipped it out of the sheath, examining its edge. "Hassún will send us to a glyph circle near the town of Zapero. There we'll take the train further into the mountains to reach Silver Valley."

He snapped the knife back into place and handed it to Boone. Hesitating, Boone took it. The leather felt cold in his grip. His legs were like jelly. "Why me?"

"Isn't that obvious?" Colorow said. "You're a dragon."

"I do not like this," Hassún said with a frown. "Evans is not completely trained. He is not prepared for such a task."

Colorow fastened the flap on his bag and swung the strap over his head. "There is no more time for training. I came out of my way to fetch Boone Evans from the Veiled Canyon. I will not succeed without him."

"What task?" Boone asked.

Hassún propelled him toward the ladder. "Katsina Colorow wants you to destroy the shard."

Boone stopped and stared at Hassún. Was the Katsina serious?

"First he must find it," Vihala added.

"The shards are well protected," Hassún said. "Perhaps we overestimate the danger."

Colorow mumbled, "I find it's seldom possible to overestimate danger."

"The shard is hidden somewhere between the Chua and Achak peaks near the town of Silver Valley," Vihala said. "Let us hope it is hidden well enough to elude a skinwalker."

"Skinwalkers, too?" Boone blurted. His mouth felt dry. "I thought they were long gone in the war with Orendos."

Hassún gave him an annoyed look. Boone blushed as Vihala turned to him.

"Evil never completely dies, young Evans. It merely bides its time until it sees new opportunity and seizes upon it." She laid a hand on Colorow's shoulder, stopping him short of the ladder. "I trust, Colorow, that you will take the necessary precautions if you encounter a skinwalker?"

Colorow nodded. "I'll send for backup, of course."

Vihala made an indelicate snort at odds with her elegant demeanor. "When did you ever ask for help, or even take it when it was offered?"

He gave a slight bow. "I have ever been your servant, Vihala."

Vihala closed her eyes. "You are both going into grave danger."

"We have no other choice, Vihala, if we will save our people."

She took a deep breath. "Then our fate rests in your hands, Colorow."

"Don't worry," Colorow said quietly. "We will not fail."

Chapter 3
Riding an Iron Horse through a Notch

G loomy weather bogged down Pa and Jesse's journey. It was a long trip to the Colorado Rockies anyway, and they were behind schedule. It was early fall by the time they got to an outpost in the foothills of the Rocky Mountains where they would catch a narrow gauge train into Silver Valley.

Jesse was anxious to see Sam again. It had been two long years since his brother left to seek his fortune in the silver mines. The few letters they'd received spoke of Sam getting married, learning to drill holes for dynamite, and being promoted to foreman at one of the big mining operations called the Bellawest.

Pa purchased tickets from a small booth at one end of the railroad platform. It was almost as big as the town it served. People dressed in their Sunday best milled around, waiting for the train to arrive. Shoes clipped across the platform boards, harnesses jingled, and people chattered.

A newspaper boy dressed in knickers and a cap hawked papers at the other end of the platform. "President Hayes relieves Storm of the Century victims!" he hollered above the din. "Read all about it!"

Jesse felt heat rise in his cheeks. He wished he could block his ears. He didn't want to hear about the tornadoes last spring.

With a shrill whistle, the train rounded a bend and pulled up to the platform in a cloud of steam and coal smoke. Pa finished buying their tickets and directed a porter to load their trunks, then led the way to one of the passenger cars.

Jesse followed until he spotted a youth on the other side of the platform no more than three years older than himself. The young man had thick auburn hair poking out from under the brim of a tan Western hat. His nose was almost too big for his face. His eyes were wide and a pale shade of blue that gave him an innocent look as he gawked at the people around him. He was tall, dressed in a leather duster that just brushed the tops of his worn boots.

All this would have been ordinary enough. Jesse would not have given the youth a second thought except for the hulking shadow surrounding him. Jesse rubbed his eyes, thinking his travels had left him more worn out than he realized.

The shadow moved exactly with the young man, as if it were a reflection of him. But it towered as tall as the train in the shape of an animal that can either walk on all fours or its hind legs. The head had an elongated snout, like drawings of an alligator Jesse had once seen in a book. Only this was much bigger than any alligator he'd imagined. The shadow had a tail that twitched back and forth behind the young man. Jesse winced as the tail swung toward the ticket booth, but it passed right through it like smoke.

The young man turned and caught Jesse staring. They looked at each other for a full minute. The youth's eyes narrowed. He turned to whisper to an Indian man standing nearby. The Indian was dressed like the youth, with a long black braid under a black hat and a shotgun slung across his back. The harsh features of the man's face seemed threatening.

Jesse swallowed hard, his throat uncomfortably dry.

"Jesse?" Pa called from the steps of the passenger car. "Come along, son."

Jesse scrambled gratefully out of range of those two pairs of eyes. It was ten minutes before he could calm the pounding of his heart.

The train sped its way into the mountains, sticking close to a cliff on one side that loomed over the tracks as if it would fall and crush the train at any moment. Jesse couldn't see anything but trees from the windows of the passenger car. As they climbed higher, more and more of the aspen leaves were a bright yellow color, glinting in the morning sun and contrasting with the dark needles of pine trees. Jesse felt like he was traveling through a tunnel that closed off any possibility of retreat.

"You gonna eat that or just play with it?" Pa asked from the seat beside him.

Jesse looked down at the apple he twisted over and over in his hands. His stomach didn't feel up to it. He handed the apple to Pa and stood up.

"I think I need some air," he said.

Pa shrugged, taking a big bite of his own apple and speaking out one side of his mouth. "Suit yourself."

Jesse climbed over Pa into the aisle. It was narrow, the ceiling low. Jesse was able to stand upright, but just barely. He made his way down the aisle to the end of the car. His stomach was in knots. He wondered if he could make it to the back platform of the caboose before he sicked up.

He had one hand on the door handle when he heard a faint gasp. His eyes searched out the source.

In the last seat to his right, a girl ducked her head. Although her long dark hair fell forward before he could get a good look at her face, he had the impression of distorted features and wrinkled skin. She was dressed smart, in a blue no-nonsense frock with a dark coat. She had blue ribbons in her hair.

Jesse hesitated. He turned the handle and started to open the door, then stopped. Moving slowly, he closed it again. His stomach no longer felt like it was about to erupt.

"Is…is something wrong, miss?" he asked.

The girl shook her head without lifting her face. "No. I'm fine." Her voice was mellow and smooth like the richest cream.

"You ain't feeling poorly or nothing? This train's got my gut in an uproar." As he heard the last words leave his mouth, he winced and mentally kicked himself. That was about the dumbest thing he could have said to a girl.

She giggled, one gloved hand flying up to cover a mouth he couldn't see. The sound was like a music box he'd heard once at the general store.

"Is this kid bothering you, Eliza?" a gruff voice asked.

Jesse turned as a hulking boy approached down the aisle. The boy had to walk sideways to fit between the seats, but he wasn't fat. Jesse thought that if he tried to plow a fist into the boy, he'd break his wrist against pure muscle.

The boy radiated hostility as he reached past Jesse to hand a sandwich wrapped in wax paper to the girl, crowding Jesse into the back door. Jesse felt small and thin.

"He isn't bothering me nearly as much as you are, Allan," the girl retorted. All the music was gone from her voice. "He was just asking after my health."

Her chin came up, causing her hair to slide back and reveal her profile. Jesse took another step back into the opposite seat. Her face was disfigured, the skin sagging like melted wax. The eye he could see had no eyebrow or lashes. He wondered if she really looked that way, or if he was again seeing things.

"What are you staring at?" Allan growled.

"N...nothing," Jesse said. Obviously, the girl—Eliza— really was disfigured.

She turned to look at him and he saw that the left side of her face was smooth, with freckles sprinkled liberally across her cheekbones, her lips full and pert. Her feisty expression was replaced by sadness.

Stumbling, Jesse got past Allan and made his way back to his seat. He slid down in it and covered his face with his hat.

"Feel better?" Pa asked.

Jesse didn't answer.

Chapter 4
Ankling In for a Sit Down

B oone and Colorow were the first to step off the train when it reached Silver Valley, almost before the train came to a full stop.

The town was bigger than Boone expected, with a roundabout to turn the train, a main street sporting the usual stores plus a ladies' hat shop, and at least twenty solid frame buildings spread across the valley from the river in the east to the mountains rising in the west. It seemed the mining business had been good to Silver Valley.

"So, we gonna follow that kid now?" Boone asked as he grabbed their bags. The boy hadn't looked like much. He was a scrawny kid with sandy hair that needed a barber and eyes too big for his narrow face. But there was something about him that caught Boone's attention, made him sit up and take notice. "I'm pretty sure he could see my dragon form."

"I don't suppose he's going anywhere fast," Colorow said. "First, we'll find a room for a few nights, and then I want to have a word with the local sheriff."

Boone followed Colorow down the main street. It was wide, with well-packed gravel and dirt. Trees were planted along both sides, probably to replace those uprooted when the town was built. They crossed the street, stepped onto the boardwalk, and walked into the general store.

A little bell tinkled on the door as they entered. Their boots echoed hollowly on the floorboards. Boone could smell leather and flour, lard and new cloth. Shelves and barrels were crowded with supplies. Licorice whips and gumballs the size of his thumb winked from glass jars on the counter.

But what caught Boone's interest more than anything was the soda fountain to the right. Three wooden stools perched in front of the counter. On the wall behind it, glass dishes winked next to bottles of syrup and cherries. The smells were tantalizing. It was all Boone could do not to push past Colorow and run to the counter.

A man came out of the back room, wiping his hands on his apron. He eyed Colorow suspiciously and asked in a guarded tone, "Can I help you?"

"We're looking for a room to rent," Colorow said.

"The saloon don't cater to Indians, but Widow Matthews runs a decent boarding house that takes in your kind."

Boone felt the color rise in his cheeks. Had the man just dared to insult a Katsina? Colorow didn't seem to notice.

The shopkeeper continued, "Just follow this road another block to the next street, then turn left. Her house is two blocks down, on the right. You can't miss it. She's got the only picket fence in town."

Colorow touched the brim of his hat. "Much obliged."

Before Colorow could leave, Boone asked in a rush, "I don't suppose you got ice cream for sale here?"

Colorow rolled his eyes.

The shopkeeper chuckled. "Don't you worry none, son. You ain't as far from civilization as you might think. I got a cold house in the back and a feller what brings me ice down from the mountaintops twice a week." He winked. "I make vanilla, strawberry, *and* chocolate."

Boone touched his hat as he'd seen Colorow do, grinning as Colorow grabbed his coat and hauled him outside.

"We are not here to buy ice cream," Colorow hissed under his breath. "Now, let's go find that Mrs. Matthews."

Boone had to scramble to keep up with Colorow as he strode down the street, following the directions the shopkeeper gave.

They passed several pedestrians and a few horses and wagons before they found a two-story clapboard house with a white picket fence circling the yard. A willow tree nearly as tall as the house grew in front, and Boone realized this must be one of the first houses built in Silver Valley.

Mrs. Matthews was a stout, handsome woman dressed in black frills and a clean white apron. As she showed them into a sitting room, Boone glimpsed two kids heading into the kitchen and thought he recognized them from the train. He hardly noticed the girl, but the hefty boy glared at Boone before disappearing behind the kitchen door.

"You're in luck, gentlemen," the woman said. "I have one more room with two beds on the second floor available for rent." She smelled like fresh bread, ginger, and cream. Boone's stomach rumbled. "And," she added, eyeing Boone, "dinner will be waiting for you in the parlor as soon as you've freshened up."

There was only one other tenant seated at the gleaming oak table when Boone and Colorow entered awhile later. She had a queenly bearing, sitting straight and tall. Her skin was fair, contrasting with ebony hair piled high on her head in the latest womanly fashion. Her dark eyes were tilted slightly upward, giving her a mischievous aura. She smelled like wild roses, and the smell brought thoughts of comfort to Boone's mind.

Mrs. Matthews bustled into the room, balancing a couple of china dishes and a basket of brown bread.

"The room is right pretty," Boone said. He blushed as he caught Colorow's stern look. "Should suit us just fine," he added in a mumble.

Mrs. Matthews smiled at Boone. "Gentlemen, please make yourselves at home. This is Miss Dalton, our local schoolteacher. Miss Dalton, may I present my newest tenants, Mr. Colorow and Mr. Evans."

Colorow gave a slow nod. "Charmed, Miss Dalton."

"Likewise, Mr. Colorow, Mr. Evans."

"I have a thick hot stew on the fire," said Mrs. Matthews. "I'd be glad to bring you all a bowl."

"Thank you, ma'am," Colorow said.

Boone perched his hat on the back of his chair, imitating Colorow, and sat down.

"I'm half starved," Boone said, reaching for a slice of bread. Colorow kicked him under the table. Boone looked over in surprise. "What?"

"Are you gentlemen miners?" Miss Dalton asked.

"No, ma'am," Boone said.

"He means, not yet," Colorow said quickly, kicking Boone under the table again. Boone was sure his leg would be covered in bruises by the end of the meal.

Mrs. Matthews re-entered with three bowls of stew on a platter.

Colorow waited to begin eating until Miss Dalton lifted the spoon delicately and sampled a mouthful. Realizing his earlier blunder at not waiting for the lady, Boone tried not to blush as he buttered a slice of bread.

Miss Dalton addressed Boone. "Surely you're too young to be a miner, aren't you, Mr. Evans? I should think you would still be in school."

"I am," Boone stammered. "That is, I don't go to a school like the one you teach, but I'm still learning."

Colorow cut in. "Aren't we all still learning? Mr. Evans is older than he looks, Miss Dalton. He's done this sort of work before."

Boone turned to stare wide-eyed at Colorow, but he didn't want another kick to the shins, so he kept quiet.

"Oh, I see," said Miss Dalton. She hesitated a minute, holding her spoon in midair before setting it down again. "I feel it only fair to warn you gentlemen."

"Warn us of what?" Colorow asked, putting down his own spoon and studying her.

Miss Dalton squirmed a little in her seat, as if the subject made her uncomfortable. She lowered her voice before she continued. "There have been a lot of mining accidents in the last several months. They have affected the parents of

31

many of my students. Although no one has been seriously injured so far, I can tell the children are worried about it. You understand, gentlemen, that I don't like to repeat rumors, but there is talk of a girl, an Indian girl, being spotted nearby whenever one of these accidents occurs. People around here began calling her the widowmaker."

"The widowmaker?" Boone asked.

"They believe she is the cause of the accidents. That she is trying to make widows of those whose loved ones work in the mines, if you will. It's just superstitious nonsense, I'm sure."

"I'm sure," Colorow said.

Miss Dalton wiped her mouth a final time and folded her napkin neatly. "I'm afraid I must leave you. The dinner hour is nearly over, and I need to ring the school bell for the afternoon session."

Colorow and Boone stood up as she did. Colorow took her hand and bowed over it as she left him with a smile. The scent of wild roses lingered in the room after she had gone.

Boone sat back down and reached for his spoon, but stopped short as Colorow cuffed him lightly on the back of the head.

"Ow!" Boone said. "What was that for?"

"Next time," said Colorow, "let me do all the talking."

"Mr. Owens?" The stout young woman who met Pa and Jesse at the station fidgeted nervously with her handbag before stepping forward to extend one gloved hand toward Pa. "I'm Mary, Sam's wife. He's working this afternoon, but he asked me to show you to your cabin."

Mary was short, even shorter than Jesse. She had a pleasant, round face with ruddy cheeks and long dark eyelashes. Her light hair was swept up into a bun under a simple hat. A green cape, frayed at the edges, was draped over her shoulders.

Pa gave her what passed for his smile these days. "I'm mighty pleased to know you, Mary."

"And this must be Jesse. You're taller than Sam described."

Jesse straightened his back and gave her a shy smile. "I've grown a mite since he last saw me."

"I'm sorry I wasn't able to meet your mother," she said.

Pa's mustache twitched. He was silent for several moments. He didn't look at Mary, just watched the porters unload luggage from the baggage car. Jesse bit his lip and looked down at his boots. The silence became awkward.

"Forgive me, Mr. Owens. I didn't mean…" Mary finally stammered.

"Yes, well," Pa said. He turned and strode toward one of their trunks. "Jesse, come help me with this."

They loaded the trunks and bags into the back of the small wagon Mary brought. Pa drove the wagon through the streets of the town according to Mary's directions. They avoided the main road, taking a side road that led to the west end of town.

Jesse stared up at the mountains looming around the valley. He couldn't see past their towering peaks. That bothered him, like an itch he couldn't reach. He wondered how long it would take to climb to the top of one of those peaks so he could get a good view of his surroundings.

They passed a white-washed church with a steeple that looked like it housed a bell. The mining must really be as rich as Sam said it was for the town to have such an elegant church building.

Pa used to tell Ma he'd rather worship the good Lord under a blue sky than under roof beams. Lines would jump around Ma's mouth every time he said things like that. She was a stickler for going to church. At her funeral, the Baptist preacher said what a pious woman she was, and that if anybody deserved to go to heaven, it was Ma. Jesse hoped that was true.

They pulled into the yard of a tiny cabin right at the end of the last street in town. The trees started just beyond the cabin where the road continued past it, curving up into a cut in the mountain that followed a river. Here, the trees grew tall and thick.

"Sam found this place for rent," Mary said. "It might need a little fixing up, but I reckon you can handle that. I'll come by and bring you supper every so often and help out with the cleaning, if you need it."

The place looked old and neglected. Weeds littered a yard inside a simple wooden fence. A small shed off to the right seemed on the verge of collapse. Small and leaning to one side, the cabin itself was poorly built. The wooden planks must have been green when they were nailed together. They shrank as they continued to dry, leaving too much space between many of the planks. It would be cold in the cabin, especially at night, until the holes were chinked.

Pa swung down and helped Mary off the wagon. "Here, son," he said as he handed the carpet bags to Jesse. "Take these on in."

Jesse followed Mary up the steps of the small porch, hoping the roof wouldn't cave in on them when they opened the door.

The smell of fresh bread wrapped him up as he walked in. Jesse stopped just inside the door and stared. A rag rug of bright colors lay on the floor, brightening the front room like a ray of sunshine. Near the door, a round dining table was set for two with a pretty lace tablecloth. Against the far wall, a hutch held crockery, what looked like food supplies, and some dishes. A wood stove radiated heat from the center of the room, where Mary removed a dishcloth to reveal a pie and a pan of fresh bread.

"I hope you like chicken pot pie," she said. She picked up a knife and cut the pie into generous portions. Jesse took a deep breath, sucking in the smell greedily.

"I can see why Sam married you," he said. Then his cheeks burned hot as he realized what he'd said.

Mary laughed. "I knew you'd be hungry when you came in. A boy your age never stops eating anyhow. I got three little brothers, and they're all stuffing their faces morning, noon, and night."

"I'll just put these bags away," Jesse mumbled. He scooted past her and slipped through a doorway to the back room.

There was one frame bed against the wall to the right in the small room he entered. A mattress stuffed with straw perched on top of ropes strung across the frame for springs. A colorful patched quilt was folded neatly at the foot of the bed.

At the opposite side of the room, a second bed was made up on the floor with another straw mattress and quilt. Jesse knew that would be his bed. A small table between the beds and next to a window held a porcelain washbasin and pitcher with little blue flowers painted on them. A small mirror hung over the table. Jesse caught his reflection in it as he entered the room. He looked haggard and grubby from the train ride.

He carried the bags across the small room to the table with the washbasin. One of the boards in the floor shifted under his boots as he set down the bags. He bent to examine it more closely. As he wriggled the board, one end came loose and tilted up. There was an open space under the floor.

Jesse looked back over his shoulder. He could hear Pa open the front door and speak to Mary. Quickly, Jesse dug the bottle out of his pocket with the dirt in it from Ma's grave. He dropped the bottle into the hole under the floor and replaced the board as best he could.

He was just standing up when the sound of boots hitting the floorboards announced Pa's arrival in the back room.

"Washin' up for dinner?" Pa asked. He set the trunk he carried down near the door.

"Yeah." Jesse tossed his hat onto his bed and poured water from the pitcher into the washbasin. He splashed it up onto his face. It cooled the heat in his cheeks.

"Mary says it's ready whenever we are." Pa took a turn at the washbasin, spluttering through the water as it splashed onto his face. "Looks like Sam picked hisself a winner with that one. Feels good to be here, don't it? Starting over."

Pa dried his hands on a nearby towel and clapped a hand on Jesse's shoulder. Jesse tried not to shrink away.

"C'mon, son. Let's eat!"

Jesse checked the loose floorboard before following Pa out of the room. It still tilted up slightly. He'd have to find a hammer soon to get it back into place. He didn't want Pa finding the bottle.

Chapter 5
Fish or Cut Bait

It was drizzling on Sunday morning. Jesse tried to wash and dress without waking Pa, but when he stubbed his toe on the washbasin and nearly tipped the china pitcher over, he gave out a yelp. Pa woke and chased him out of the room, hollering that Jesse should go pester somebody else.

Sam had visited them the night before. Jesse was shocked at how much older Sam looked in the three years since they'd seen each other. Two weeks' of beard growth and lingering dirt from Sam's mining shift didn't help.

Sam and Pa stayed up late into the night, talking. Some hours after dark, Jesse gave up on them and went to bed. On the way, he asked Pa if they could attend church services the next day. Pa was surprised, but said Jesse could go with Sam and Mary if he had a hankering for punishment.

Jesse managed to get into his best trousers and a clean shirt without bothering Pa again and set off to walk the short distance to the church.

The preacher stood near the door, shaking hands and welcoming folks as they arrived.

"Well, now, here's a new face," he said, holding out a hand as Jesse approached. "I'm Reverend Hall. You must be the new boy from down the road that Mary Owens told me about."

Jesse took the reverend's hand. "Jesse," he mumbled.

"Is your father joining us today?"

"Not today," Jesse said.

"Well, I guess you can tell him about the sermon later. Come in; find yourself a seat. We'll get started here in just a few minutes."

Jesse entered a small entryway that opened into the chapel. There were about ten pews on both sides of an aisle. The pews were covered in red velvet cushions, with little hymnals in slots on the back of each pew. Four tall stained-glass windows lined the walls of the church, depicting scenes from the Bible and creating a warm, even glow. In the front of the chapel, a woman pumped vigorously on an organ, filling the small room with mellow sound. An embroidered cross hung on the wall behind a podium.

The chapel smelled of new wood and freshly brewed coffee. It brought a wave of homesickness over Jesse. Not counting the funeral, the last time he'd been in church was with Ma the Sunday before she died.

Jesse thought he recognized the girl from the train and the boy who had been with her sitting on the front row to the right next to a plump woman who must be their mother. The girl glanced over her shoulder as Jesse came in, saw him, and quickly turned back around.

Mary and Sam sat in the fourth row to the left. Mary saw Jesse and waved. Sam looked sleepy and out of sorts, but he nodded politely to Jesse as Jesse sat down next to him.

Reverend Hall gave a rousing sermon, as far as sermons go. There were a couple of times when Jesse was sure the roof would fly off the building. At least it kept him awake, but he fidgeted the entire time in spite of the annoyed looks he got from Sam. Jesse remembered why he'd always complained so much when Ma dragged him to church.

Jesse had never been so glad to hear a church bell in his life as when the sermon finally ended and the sexton rang the bell. Mary and Sam walked Jesse home. It had stopped raining, though clouds still lowered overhead. Jesse tugged at his collar and unbuttoned the top button so he could breathe.

"There's a lake about half a mile up the road from your cabin," Sam said as they walked. He seemed to be in a better mood himself now that services were over. "It's called Crystal Lake, on account of the water being so clear. Best fishing for miles."

Jesse's mood lightened considerably. "Can we go fishing, Sam?"

Sam hesitated. "If it's okay with Mary."

Mary smiled. "Go on with you. Take the boy fishing."

Sam ruffled Jesse's hair before Jesse could jerk his head away. "Looks like we're on, Little Sprout."

"I'm thirteen now, Sam. You don't have to call me 'Little Sprout' anymore."

He chuckled. "Just Sprout, then."

Jesse scowled at him.

Pa was up when they got back to the cabin and helped collect fishing gear, offering to go with them. When they reached the lake, Jesse left Pa and Sam on the east side and made his way around to the north, looking for his own spot to fish.

Tall fir and pine trees crowded around the lake and made the going tough at times, but he soon found a good spot on a knoll overlooking a deep pool. Jesse nestled against a tree trunk and set his line. He pulled the pole back and whipped it forward so the line flew out over the water and fell gracefully in an arc, hitting the surface with a small plunk.

There was an island covered in rock and trees in the middle of the lake. The water was so still, it reflected the trees around it and the mountain peaks towering on all sides. The sun broke through the clouds and glinted off the water.

Jesse had to admit to himself that the scene was beautiful, even if he couldn't see past the mountain peaks. It was a shame Ma had never seen this place. She would have loved it. The thought made Jesse feel sad and he pushed it away, settling back into the tree trunk and closing his eyes.

Sometime later, he felt a raindrop hit his arm. He tipped his hat back, looking up at the sky. The clouds had closed back in. Rain would rouse the fish into biting, but it made the waiting more miserable. Still, it would be worth it to see what Mary could do with a good catch. He hunkered down beneath the tree and prepared for a long haul.

Boone watched Colorow pull the harness for his rifle off the coat rack and strap it across his chest.

They were in the room they shared in Mrs. Matthews' home. It was a large room with two single beds, a dormer window, and a writing desk.

Boone lounged on his bed, hands behind his head and boots off so he wouldn't muddy Mrs. Matthews' frilly pink coverlet. There was a matching coverlet on Colorow's bed and a vase of fresh flowers on the small table between the beds, not to mention the lacy window curtains. Womenfolk had peculiar notions about decorating.

Colorow picked up his rifle from the desk and slid it smoothly into the harness.

"That's a rare rifle you got there," Boone said. "Dragon-made, ain't it?"

Colorow grunted in reply.

Boone stood up and slipped his feet into his boots. "My uncle used to make weapons, I hear. But nobody's seen him in a few centuries." He reached for his hat on the coatrack, but Colorow stopped him.

"I'm going to talk to a few townsfolk and buy some supplies for the investigation," he said. "You are not coming with me."

"What? What am I supposed to do in the meantime?"

"You're horrible at glyphs. Maybe you could practice for once."

Boone rubbed the bridge of his nose. Glyphs were boring. He'd always had a hard time interpreting the dragon writing the Katsina used for communication and spells. Besides, he needed to prove himself somehow so Colorow would confide in him. "You want I should check out that kid we saw on the train?"

Colorow gave him a steady stare until Boone grew uncomfortable. "You asking for trouble, Boone?"

"I just want to find out if I'm right about him seeing my true form."

"No. What if you're wrong, and he can't? You'd tip our hand."

"So I'd be stealthy about it, careful-like."

"That won't work unless I hog-tie your mouth."

Boone frowned. "Sorry about downstairs already. I'll be more careful."

"See that you are." Colorow grabbed his hat and opened the door. "Fine. You can keep an eye on the boy, but don't talk to him, and don't let him see you in dragon form. I'll be back by nightfall."

Jesse caught three nice-sized trout and a small bass before he started walking back to the spot where he'd left Sam and Pa. As he got nearer, he could hear them talking and soon made out the words. He stopped.

"...been wrecking things," Pa said. "Last thing was the chicken coop. Durndest thing I ever saw. I don't know where he got that much ice to freeze a whole coop like that."

"The chickens?" Sam asked.

Pa's voice sounded weary. Jesse could imagine him running a hand across his eyes. "Froze, I guess. He won't talk to me, just sulks around the house all the time. I wish your ma was here. She'd know what to do. I just don't." His voice broke on the last words.

Sam sounded tight, controlled. "We all wish Ma was still here. Don't fret. Things'll get better. Jesse'll toe the line or I'll know the reason why not."

A shadow swept over Jesse from above. He looked up, expecting to see a bird. Something red and huge disappeared into the trees at least half a mile behind him near the lake's edge.

Jesse realized his jaw was clenched. He made an effort to relax. Pa and Sam were still talking, but he was no longer interested in what they had to say. He put the fish and gear down quietly against a rock and turned, heading for the trees where he'd seen the red thing disappear.

It was getting cold and dark. The cloud cover brought on night even earlier than normal in this high place ringed with mountains. At home in Kansas, there'd be another hour of daylight at least.

Jesse slowed as he got near the trees where he'd seen the red thing fall. He peered into the dark shadows. At first he couldn't make anything out. Then he thought he could see two eyes, blinking at him from the darkness.

He swallowed hard and forced the butterflies in his stomach to hold still. "I see you there," he called, "so don't bother hiding."

A voice cussed from the direction of the eyes. "Humans ain't supposed to look up."

Jesse thought about running away. He could fetch Pa and Sam, but by then the creature he'd seen would be gone. Instead, Jesse forced his legs forward. Now he could make out the owner of those eyes. It was the youth he'd seen at the train station. The huge ghostly form still loomed around him, like a hole in the shadow of the trees. Jesse's fear drained away into curiosity.

"What are you?" he asked.

The boy smirked. "Don't you mean, 'Who are you?'"

Jesse looked up at the shadow surrounding the boy. "No, I mean *what* are you? I reckon I might be crazy, but I see…something hovering around you."

"I knew it!" A grin split his face in two like a ripe watermelon. "I told Colorow you could see my true form."

Jesse took a step back, trying to contain his shock. Did the boy mean the shadow around him was real?

"Thanks for not screaming," continued the boy. "You must be one gutsy kid."

"Kid?" Jesse bristled. "I ain't much younger than you. How old are you?"

"Two hundred and fifty, give or take a decade."

Jesse blinked. "What?"

"Dragons live longer than humans, but if'n you converted that to human years, I reckon I'm close to your age."

"Are you telling me you're a dragon?"

"The genuine article. Of course, you probably ain't never heard of dragons before, have you?"

Jesse studied the shadow above the boy. "Is it like an alligator?"

The boy snorted. "Not even close. I'm Boone, by the way. Boone Evans."

"Jesse Owens."

Jesse hesitated, then took the hand the boy offered and shook. Boone's grip was firm, normal. There wasn't anything frightening about his easy-going manner or his wide smile. Jesse felt more comfortable.

Boone tipped his hat back and scratched at his gingery hair. "I'm probably gonna get in a heap of trouble for this," he said. "I ain't supposed to talk to you. But since I'm yammering anyhow, can I ask you a question?"

"You just did."

"Right." Boone blushed a shade that nearly matched his hair. "Another question."

Jesse pursed his lips together to squelch a smile. "Shoot."

"Have you seen any other strange things lately—besides me, that is?"

"Why?"

"Curious, you might say."

Jesse thought about all the strange things that had happened since Ma died. He put on a bland expression and shrugged. "Not unless you count being a thousand miles from home."

Boone studied him for a few minutes. "And home would be—?"

"Randolph, Kansas."

"Whew! You are a long way from home." He looked around at the gathering gloom. "Well, it's nearly dark. I'd best be getting back, or my..." He seemed to change what he was about to say. "My tutor will get after me."

"You have a tutor?"

Boone grimaced. "Unfortunately. By the way, you'd best not mention any of this to your pa. He might not take kindly to talk of a dragon in the neighborhood."

"He'd say I'd fallen off my rocker."

"Yeah, that too. Be seeing you around, Jesse."

He walked away through the trees without looking back, strolling casually just as if he didn't have a giant shadowy tail swinging along behind him.

Chapter 6
Kicking Up a Row

P a took Jesse to the town's one-room schoolhouse the next morning. The teacher was a pretty woman decked out in a gray tailored dress with long sleeves, a high collar, and buttons down the front. A watch was pinned to the bodice. Her jet-black hair was pulled back into a bun, making her forehead look higher. She smiled kindly at them.

"I'm Miss Dalton," she said when Pa introduced themselves. "We're glad to have you with us, Jesse. I'll ring the school bell shortly to call in the other children. In the meantime, you can be seated here in the middle of this row."

Jesse hesitated, looking over at Pa.

Pa clapped a hand on Jesse's shoulder. "Send for Mary if you need anything, son. I'll be at the Bellawest mine all day, starting my new job," He followed the teacher out the door.

The school had a high ceiling. A blackboard dominated the wall in front of Jesse with a teacher's desk off to the side. Paintings of United States presidents decorated the walls. The desks each sat two children and were lined up neatly in three rows, four desks to a row. Jesse sat gingerly down in the desk farthest to the left, kitty-corner from the teacher's desk and closest to the window.

A handful of children of varying ages played in the yard around the school. As the bell rang in a steady cadence, the children stopped their play and ran toward the schoolhouse.

Jesse scanned the faces of the children as they came tumbling in the door at the back of the room. Boone didn't appear, but Allan did. When Allan came in, his eyes roved the room and stopped on Jesse. A frown leaped onto his face. Jesse spun in his seat as Allan started up his aisle. Before he got all the way around, Jesse thought he saw Eliza seated at the last desk on the far side of the room. It was dark in that corner and her head was down, but he recognized the blue ribbons in her hair.

"Well, look who it is," Allan hissed from behind Jesse. "I'm warning you now, clodhopper. Stay away from my sister, d'you hear?"

A seat creaked, and Jesse risked a glance to his right to see Allan slump into the desk on the next row, three seats back. Jesse closed his eyes and dropped his head into his arms on top of his desk. He was not off to a good start.

"Children!" Miss Dalton said crisply as she swept up the middle aisle to the front of the room. "I want you all to meet our new pupil."

Jesse took a deep breath and stood up. He kept his gaze on the top of his desk.

"This is Jesse Owens," Miss Dalton said. "He has just moved here from Randolf, Kansas. Everyone, please say hello to Jesse."

The class halfheartedly chorused a "hello."

"I hope you children will introduce yourselves to Jesse during recess today and make him feel welcome."

As Jesse sat back down, he could feel the eyes of the other children drilling into him.

Miss Dalton handed him a book. "Before we begin, I want to remind you of the community fall picnic this Sunday around Crystal Lake. Everyone is invited, so encourage your parents to pack a picnic lunch and attend. Now, will you please open your readers to page twenty-three? Ruthanne, begin reading at the top of the page."

As a girl three rows over started reading in a dreadful monotone, Miss Dalton moved closer to her, bending over to correct her on every other word. Jesse stared at the words on the page in front of him, but they didn't register in his brain.

Suddenly, he felt something hard hit the back of his neck. He put up a hand and came away with a crumbling bit of chalk. Jesse glanced over his shoulder. Allan waved a peashooter at him before sliding it into his desk. The boy sitting next to him grinned wickedly at Jesse.

Then Jesse noticed that Eliza was also watching him. The disfigured side of her face was away from him and in shadow. She was pretty, seen from this side, and her eyes were clear and bright.

"Jesse Owens?"

Jesse snapped back to attention and realized Miss Dalton had been repeating his name.

"Is there a problem?" she asked.

"No, ma'am." He swallowed hard as he looked up at her.

"Then perhaps you will read the next paragraph for us?"

Jesse stared down at the book in front of him, feeling sweat break out on his brow and his cheeks grow hot.

"Wh…where are we?"

The class sniggered. Jesse wanted to melt and slide away under the door.

Later, at recess, Jesse sat on the steps of the schoolhouse, wondering what had happened to Miss

Dalton's suggestion that the other children make Jesse feel welcome.

Most of the boys ignored him as they got together a game of baseball. The girls either ignored Jesse as well or stared at him like he was some rare species of a particularly ugly spider. Jesse longed for his school friends back home in Kansas, but he was afraid he would never see them again.

Allan came up to bat to the roaring cheers of his teammates. It seemed he was well liked in the school. He picked up the bat and turned to the side, ready to swing. The first pitch went wide, and the boy acting as umpire called a ball. As Jesse watched Allan get ready for the second pitch, Jesse slowly became aware of voices coming from the other side of the schoolyard.

"...surprised your momma lets you come to school at all," came a boy's voice.

Jesse looked around for the source and spotted a group of older boys clustered around something against the fence in the farthest corner of the yard.

"She probably wants to get you outta the house so's you won't curdle the cream." Another boy laughed.

Jesse looked around. Miss Dalton was inside the schoolhouse. The other children continued playing as if they couldn't hear the rude remarks.

Jesse stood up and started walking toward the knot of boys. He noticed a girl stumble on her skipping rope when she saw Jesse moving that direction. Her eyes widened, and she shook her head slightly. Jesse ignored her. He kept his eyes on the group of boys.

There were three of them, all burly and tall. Their backs were to Jesse, so they didn't see him coming as they stared down at whoever crouched behind them against the fence.

"I'm getting sick just looking at you," sneered a third boy. He reached down and scooped up a handful of mud. "This oughtta cover that ugly mug of yours."

Before Jesse knew what had happened, he was beside the boy, grabbing the arm with the mud. The boy looked back, surprised, as Jesse's grip kept him from flinging the mud onto Eliza.

She huddled against the fence, her face buried in her arms, as far away from the boys as she could get. She looked small and vulnerable, like a sparrow caught in a fox's den. Jesse could see her shaking.

One of the boys frowned at Jesse. "You looking for trouble, new kid?"

"You're the ones who'll find trouble," Jesse said, "if her brother catches you."

"I ain't afraid of Allan." The boy shook his arm free of Jesse's grasp. He was easily as large as Allan and towered over Jesse. "He should get his freak sister out of here. We don't want her here."

Jesse tightened his fists, the nails digging painfully into the palms. A sudden crack of lightning almost directly overhead made them all jump. The boys looked up at the clouds.

"Looks like the storm's moving back in," Allan's voice said from behind them. He sauntered up to the group, still holding the bat perched on his shoulder. "You should clear out, Zeke."

Zeke turned to Allan and placed his fists on his hips. "Who's gonna make me?"

There was another crack of thunder.

"Children!" Miss Dalton's voice came from the school door. "The weather has turned. Please come inside right away." She began to ring the bell.

Zeke grinned maliciously. "Saved by the bell."

He and his friends headed for the schoolhouse, pushing past Allan and knocking him in the shoulder. Jesse thought for a minute that Allan would swing the bat at Zeke, but then he threw it down and turned on Jesse.

"What do you think you're doing, sticking your big nose into other people's business?" Allan snapped.

Jesse stared at him, his mouth working. "I...I was only trying to help."

Allan strode past Jesse. "Well, next time, don't bother."

He reached Eliza and gently put a hand on her shoulder. She hissed, and Allan stepped back. As Eliza raised her head, still keeping her face turned away from them, Jesse realized she was shaking with anger.

"Get hold of yourself, Eliza," Allan whispered. He turned to glare at Jesse. "Ain't you going inside with the others?"

"I...I..."

"Go on, get out of here!"

Jesse turned and ran. As he stumbled toward the steps, the clouds opened into a downpour that drenched him moments before he made it into the schoolroom. He didn't see Allan or Eliza the rest of the day.

Chapter 7
You Can't Resist a Piece of Calico

B oone grumbled as he pulled on the stiff coveralls Colorow had bought in the general store. "Why me?"

"Quit your griping," Colorow said. "I thought dragons liked being underground."

"That's news to me. I'll get dirty."

"A little dirt never hurt anybody." Colorow held out a plain gray cap with a gaslight on it. "You'll need this."

Boone snorted. "What's wrong with my hat? I had it made special in Philadelphia. It's a genuine Stetson Boss of the Plains, with holes for my horns and everything."

"Then I don't suppose you want to risk it getting ruined. Besides, you need a light down there."

"I can see in the dark just fine."

"Not underground you can't, not without the moon, the stars. Here." Colorow shoved the hat at him.

Boone reluctantly removed his Stetson and set it carefully on the bed. He jammed the cap down low over his eyes.

They had been in Silver Valley for three days, asking around casually about the mining accidents. So far, their luck at getting information was running about as clear as a cow pond. Colorow had decided it was time for some undercover work.

"Now remember," said Colorow, "ask around about the mining accidents—what happened, where, and anything anyone knows about this 'widowmaker.' I need as many details as you can get. But don't be obvious about it. Don't let your mouth run away with you, and don't talk to the same men twice. We don't want anyone getting suspicious."

"I still don't see why you can't just ask the sheriff all this."

"Because it's better to get it from the horse's mouth. Those men at the Ulay—and the other mines, for that matter—know exactly what's going on around here."

"And where are you gonna be while I'm mucking out rock with a shovel?"

"Oh, you won't be using a shovel." Colorow flashed a rare smile. "I got you on a drilling team. I told them you were a genius with a double jack, in spite of your age."

"What? I don't even know what that is!"

Colorow held out a coat and Boone slid his arms into it. "One man holds a steel chisel where they want the black powder to go. You just have to pound the chisel into the rock with a sledge hammer while the shaker, the man holding the chisel, turns it. That drills a hole in the rock for the blasting powder. I figured it was right up your alley, with your dragon strength and all. Just don't smash your partner's hands in the process."

Boone hunched down inside the coat. This job was getting worse by the minute.

There was a knock at their door. They both turned to look, as if they could see through it.

"Yes?" Colorow finally said.

Mrs. Matthews's voice was muffled. "Mr. Colorow, the sheriff is downstairs, asking to see you."

Colorow's eyebrows climbed into his hairline. "Oh, really?" He opened the door.

Mrs. Matthew stood on the landing, wringing her hands. "I hope there isn't any trouble, Mr. Colorow," she said with a worried frown. "I run a clean establishment, and I don't hold with law breaking."

"Don't worry, Mrs. Matthews," Colorow said. "The sheriff is an old friend. Probably just popped in to say hello." Boone marveled at how easily the lie slipped off Colorow's tongue.

They made their way down to the sitting room. It was furnished like the rest of the house, in lacy doilies and fresh flowers. A cheerful fire crackled in the white marble fireplace, taking the chill off the room. A couple of wingback chairs perched on either side of a large picture window looking out on the front yard. A settee with pink roses in the fabric squatted opposite them. A man sat gingerly on the edge of the settee, looking like a moose in a flower field.

He was a heavy man, his bulk made up of muscle more than fat. He had a bushy mustache that matched his gray brows. His skin looked like worn leather stretched to the breaking point. He held a brown hat in his hands and wore a patched vest with a shiny silver star.

He stood up as Colorow and Boone entered.

"Sheriff Picket," Colorow said, extending his hand. "How can I be of service?"

The sheriff ignored the offered hand. His face seemed to be set in a permanent frown. "You and your boy can come on down to my office with me. I got a few questions that need answers."

"Jesse, will you stay after a moment, please?" Miss Dalton's request froze Jesse's insides.

He hung back as the other children grabbed jackets from pegs near the door and ran outside. When they were gone,

Miss Dalton sat down in a desk opposite Jesse. He didn't look at her, but just stared at his boots.

"I've noticed over the last couple of days that you're struggling a bit with reading," she said softly. "Do you know what grade level you reached in your old school?"

Jesse shrugged.

"I'd like to talk with your father about getting you some extra tutoring. Could I walk home with you?"

"Pa ain't there. He works the day shift at the Bellawest."

"Of course. Perhaps I could speak with Mrs. Owens."

Jesse felt a rush of cold go through him. He looked up at her, eyes wide. Didn't she know Ma was dead?

Miss Dalton must have realized her error. Her cheeks colored, and she hastened to add, "I mean, your sister-in-law. Perhaps she could give you some extra help with your homework, or find someone who could..." She didn't finish the sentence, biting her lip as she stared at him. The expression looked odd on her pretty face.

A voice came from behind them. "Miss Dalton?"

Miss Dalton jumped a little, turning to stare into the corner. "Oh! Eliza. I didn't see you there. Why haven't you gone home? Your mother will worry."

Eliza stepped forward into the half-light between the shadows and the door. The ruined side of her face was turned away from them. "I'd be glad to help Jesse with his homework."

"Yes." Miss Dalton took a deep breath, standing up briskly. "That would do nicely. Eliza is a very adept pupil. I believe she will be able to help you, Jesse, if you let her."

Eliza held out her hand to Jesse. "Walk me home?"

It was only a few blocks from the schoolhouse to Eliza's house. The autumn weather was cool, with a light drizzle falling on Jesse's hat and raincoat. It had been raining much of the time since they'd arrived in Silver Valley three days ago. He didn't like it. It was much wetter and muddier than Kansas.

They neared a two-story house that looked like it belonged on a picture postcard, complete with a white picket fence. Instead of crossing the street to it, Eliza pulled Jesse up against another building in the shadow of a doorway.

Three people were coming out of the house across the street. Jesse recognized Boone and the tough-looking Indian Boone had been with at the train station, but there was a third man with them. He was stocky, with a star gleaming on his vest. Jesse figured he must be the local sheriff.

"Have you ever seen them before?" Eliza whispered.

Jesse hesitated. "Not the sheriff, but I seen the other two at the train station before we come up here to Silver Valley."

She turned to peer at him. "You didn't notice anything strange about them?"

Jesse's eyes flicked to Boone, to the shape of a giant alligator head hovering high above him as he turned to follow the two men down the street. "No. Why?"

"Nothing. I guess I'm just not used to strangers is all."

Jesse thought that was odd, considering she lived in a mining town and her mother ran a boarding house.

"C'mon," Eliza said. "Mother always has a fresh batch of cookies ready after school."

"What about Allan? Won't he get mad if he sees me?"

"Allan runs errands in the afternoon for the telegraph office. He won't be back until supper time. Besides, you have a good excuse to be here. I'm helping you with schoolwork."

"Oh. Right."

Eliza started across the street. Jesse watched Boone and the other men disappear around a corner before he followed Eliza into her house.

The smell of gingerbread cookies washed over him as they stepped inside.

"Mother!" Eliza called. "I'm home."

She led Jesse into the kitchen and handed him a huge gingerbread cookie from a crockery jar on the sideboard. The cookie was moist and chewy and Jesse would have liked to grab a handful, but after taking a cookie for herself, Eliza clapped the lid back on the jar and led him into the sitting room.

She kicked off her shoes, plopped down on the davenport, and tucked her feet up beneath her legs, her long dress covering them and half the davenport as well. Jesse noticed that she kept the good side of her face turned toward him as he sat in a wingback chair beside a large window that overlooked the front yard.

Jesse finished the last of his cookie and watched Eliza take a large bite of hers. "Your ma's a good cook," he said.

Eliza smiled. "The best. Papa used to say she could win the heart of the devil himself with her lemon meringue pie. Everybody in town knows this is the best place for room and board because of Mother's cooking."

"Does your pa work in the mines?"

Eliza's face fell, and she dropped her hands into her lap with the half-eaten cookie. "Papa..." She hesitated. "He died about five months ago. A fever."

The room felt colder. Jesse squirmed in his seat. "I'm sorry." It had been four months since Ma died. Eliza had lost her father not long before that.

A woman appeared in the doorway, holding a basket of clothing. She was plump, with a youthful face, and black curls escaping from her dark cap. She wore a black dress with a white apron pinned to the front. Jesse could see her resemblance to the good side of Eliza's face.

Jesse hopped to his feet, spilling his schoolbag on the floor. He bent down, trying to scoop everything back up as Eliza moved from the couch to help him.

"Don't fret over that," Mrs. Matthews said. "Introduce me to your new friend, 'Liza."

"Yes, Mother. This is Jesse Owens. He just moved here."

"Well, Jesse, I expect you'll stay for supper. We're having rib roast and potatoes."

Jesse looked up with sudden panic. "Allan?" he squeaked.

"'Liza's brother is a friendly boy," Mrs. Matthews said. "You'll get along fine, I'm sure. 'Liza, I'm going upstairs to make these beds, and then I'll need your help in the kitchen."

"Yes, ma'am," Eliza replied.

When she was gone, Jesse whispered, "Allan won't take kindly to me staying for supper."

Eliza shoved another book into his bag. "Now that Papa's gone, Allan thinks he has to hover over me all the time. Well, I can take care of myself, and I can choose my

66

own friends. C'mon." She picked up his reader and led the way to the davenport. "Let's go over the reading lesson from class today."

Chapter 8
A Lick and a Promise

The sheriff led Colorow and Boone to a small brick building with a tall metal cage outside that was just big enough for one man to lie down.

"Just had that jail cell shipped in from St. Louis," the sheriff said. "Came in on the same train you boys arrived on. Ain't that coincidental?"

He opened the door to the building and led them inside, waving them to take a seat across from his desk. Boone and Colorow remained standing.

"Suppose you tell us what this is all about, Sheriff Picket," Colorow said.

The sheriff sat down behind his desk, staring up at them as he steepled his fingers together in front of his lips. Boone felt like a horse at an auction.

Boone leaned back against the frame of the door, trying to look as tough as Colorow, and as unconcerned about a sheriff hauling them into his office. "Are we in some kind of trouble?" he asked.

The sheriff's eyes flicked to Boone, then returned to Colorow. "I hear tell you've been asking questions around town. Questions about things folks don't like to think much about. You mind telling me what an Indian is doing here in Silver Valley? And don't give me some cock-and-bull story about how you're honest workers. Them clothes are brand-spanking new, and you boys don't have the hungry look of miners about you."

Colorow pulled open his coat and reached into his pocket. "I see you're an observant man," he said. He pulled out a small leather case and flipped it open to reveal a silver marshal badge. He held it out to the sheriff. "Recognize this?"

Sheriff Picket chewed at his mustache for a moment before replying. "A U.S. marshal. I might have known you was up to no good."

"I was planning to visit you this afternoon anyway, Sheriff," Colorow said. He stuffed the badge back into his pocket. "I've been sent to investigate the mining accidents going on in this town."

Boone noticed Colorow didn't mention who had sent him, nor did he confirm that he was a U.S. marshal. He simply let Sheriff Picket jump to his own conclusions.

"I don't need the feds or no Indian sticking their noses into my business," Sheriff Picket said. "Mining's a dangerous occupation. Accidents happen. Can't be helped."

"Twelve accidents in five months?" Colorow sneered. "That's a bit beyond the normal amount, wouldn't you say?"

"Nobody's been killed."

"So far."

"And we're planning to enforce safety measures at the bigger mining operations."

"It won't be enough."

Boone piped up, "What about the widowmaker?"

Sheriff Picket's eyes narrowed as he looked at Boone. "What 'widowmaker'?"

"You know, the one everybody gossips about."

Colorow took a step forward and leaned on the desk. "Yes, Sheriff. What about this widowmaker?"

"You mean the story of some Indian girl who shows up at the site of every accident?"

"That's the one."

He blew out his mustache. "Superstitious gossip."

"So you haven't investigated it?"

"I didn't say that. It's just that I didn't find anything. The first person who saw her wasn't exactly right in the head, if you take my meaning. Then everybody else thinks they seen her when it was really a tree or a rock or something just because they've heard the story. You know how these rumors spread in a small town."

Colorow straightened. "Who was this man first claiming to see the widowmaker?"

"Wasn't a man. It was old Mad Madge. She's always off in the mountains, looking to strike it rich on some hidden gold cache or another." The sheriff leaned back in his chair, hands behind his head. "I don't see how you'll find her, not until snow falls and drives her back into town."

"She comes into town for supplies, doesn't she?"

Sheriff Picket shrugged. "I reckon, once in a while."

"Then I'll catch up to her sooner or later."

"I'm betting on later."

Colorow turned and headed for the door with Boone right behind him. "I'll take that bet. Good day, Sheriff."

Once they were back outside, Boone had to trot to keep up with Colorow. It was still raining, and mud splattered up on his new coveralls. He frowned down at it, then remembered it was only the first of what promised to be a lot of grime if he still had to go into the mines.

"Stubborn son of a gun," Colorow grumbled.

"He can't go talking to you that way!" Boone kicked at a rock. "Why didn't you just blast him with a dose of Katsina power?"

Colorow's frown turned to wry amusement. "Oh, don't worry. He will get what's coming to him soon enough. That sherriff thinks he's the lord of this little town. We'll show him. We're going to find that mining woman so fast, it will make his head spin."

"How're we going to do that?"

"Boone, it is time for you to use your unique talents."

"Don't tell me I gotta go underground now."

"No. I'll send word you can't make it today after all."

"Hallelujah!"

"Don't get too excited. You're going in there tomorrow—I still need that information. But today, I have something else in mind."

Boone felt a small thrill of excitement. So far, all he'd done was follow Colorow around like a lost puppy. "What do you want I should do?" he asked eagerly.

"I need that golden sniffer of yours. I want you to track down this mining woman so we can question her."

"Mad Madge? But the sheriff said she could be anywhere in these mountains. I wouldn't know where to start."

"Then we'd better *find* you a place to start."

By now, they were coming up on the main street. Colorow stopped at the edge of the boardwalk and pointed to the general store. "Go in there. Ask the store owner about this Madge. See if you can find out when she was last in town, if she said anything about where she was headed. But most important, find out if she traded anything to the store. You need a scent to start with."

Boone grinned. "Good thinking. What are you gonna do?"

"I'll go to the assayer's office and do the same thing. This Madge is a miner. Her first stop in town would be the assayer's office to trade in whatever precious metal she found in the mountains."

Boone nodded. "Meet you back here."

They split up, headed for different ends of the street.

As soon as Boone stepped into the general store, he caught a whiff of ice cream. His mouth started watering. A kid with sandy hair sat at the counter, woofing down a bowl of vanilla with chocolate sauce and a cherry on top.

Boone ground his teeth and tried to ignore the ice cream counter, going instead to a shelf stocked with mining supplies. He racked his brain for a casual way to bring questions about Madge into a conversation with the store owner.

"Can I help you?" The man Boone had met in here a few days ago approached from behind a counter.

"Yes," Boone said slowly. "I'm looking for supplies. I, uh, I'm planning to try my luck out in the mountains— before the snow sets in, you see."

The store owner looked him up and down, one eyebrow raised. His bald head glistened in the light of the gas lamps along the wall. "Have you ever mined before, son?" he asked.

Boone bit his lip. "No, sir. At least, not by myself," he added hastily, remembering that Colorow had made him out to be some sort of super-jack-something-or-another. "I don't suppose there are any old timers around willing to show me the ropes?"

"If you're looking to go it on your own, you don't want nobody around to take all the spoils," the store owner said.

Boone frowned as the opening he'd given the store owner to talk about Madge didn't work.

The store owner picked up a hefty coil of rope. "You'll want some good rope. Can't be without that. And some pots and pans, and foodstuffs, unless you plan on living off the land."

Boone decided to try being less subtle. "I heard talk around town of a gal, name of Madge or something. Maybe she could give me some pointers."

The store owner stared at Boone, eyes going wide. "Mad Madge?" He let out a snort. "She's crazy as a hoot owl— thinks the whole mountainside belongs to her. She'd sooner shoot you in the gut than help you find any hidden gold around here."

"Well, have you seen her around lately?"

"I ain't seen Madge since the start of summer." He scratched at his head. "Come to think of it, she should have been down by now for supplies. She's crazy, but I don't like to think of something bad happening to her."

"What kind of supplies does she usually buy? Does she trade you for them, in kind?"

The store owner frowned at Boone. "Madge don't have anything worth trading. What are you so interested in her for? You ain't figuring on following her out to one of her claims, are you?"

Boone turned quickly to the mining supplies, grabbing the rope the store keeper had suggested. "I ain't a claim jumper, mister. I'm just getting ideas to help me look for my own claim, that's all. I'll take this rope for now."

He held it out.

The store owner still seemed suspicious. "That'll be seventy-five cents."

Boone fished in his pocket. Colorow had given him some pocket money earlier in the week. He handed the store owner the coins and started for the door.

The smell of ice cream stopped him. He'd nearly forgotten about it. The sandy-haired kid was just licking up the last of his ice cream. He laid a coin on the counter and hopped up from the stool. "Thanks, Mr. Clements," the kid said.

"Sure thing, Zeke," the store owner replied. "Just see you don't spend all your pocket change on ice cream or I'll get a tongue-lashing from your ma."

The kid grinned mischievously and left the store.

Boone took another step toward the door and stopped again. He breathed in deeply. Then he peered over at the counter, trying to see the coin Zeke had left. But Mr. Clements picked it up and swept away the dirty dish, wiping down the counter with a cloth.

Boone licked his lips. "How much was that dish of ice cream?" he asked.

The shopkeeper looked up in surprise. "Ice cream? Oh, that's right. You were interested in that before, when you come in the shop a few days ago with that Indian fellow. Ice cream is two pennies a scoop, one penny extra for toppings."

Boone was at the counter in three long strides. "Never mind the toppings. I'll take five scoops of vanilla...for starters."

Eliza proved to be a patient tutor, gently correcting Jesse when he made a mistake and pouring on the praise when he did it right. After a while, he no longer noticed the misshapen wrinkles on the right side of her face.

When it was time to fix supper, Mrs. Matthews discovered she was out of eggs. "Jesse," she said, "would you be a dear and run into town to the general store?"

Jesse couldn't fathom buying eggs at a store, but he took the dime and the basket Mrs. Matthews gave him and headed for Main Street. It was a short walk. The rain had stopped for now, but there were still muddy puddles everywhere. Jesse splashed through one of them, just to see how high the water would shoot.

When Jesse stepped into the store, he looked around at the rows of supplies, trying to spot the eggs. Then his eye fell on a soda counter to the right. Boone sat at one of the stools, his back to Jesse, scooping something into his mouth from a dish on the counter.

"Can I help you, son?" the store owner asked as he came around the ice cream counter. "What are you looking for?"

Jesse tore his eyes off Boone. "I…I need some eggs. For Mrs. Matthews."

"Sure thing. Just a minute."

Boone turned to peer over his shoulder at Jesse. His face was covered in different colors of ice cream. He grinned. "Hey there, kid."

Jesse thought Boone was the one who looked like a kid, with ice cream smeared all over his face.

Boone patted the stool next to him. "Have a sit down. George!" he hollered. "Bring me another, and one for my friend here." He peered at Jesse as Jesse stepped hesitantly forward. "You want chocolate or strawberry? I think I ate all the vanilla."

The store owner came over from the other counter, holding a basket of eggs. "How many?"

Shrugging, Jesse handed over his dime.

"That'll buy a dozen." He counted out the eggs into Jesse's basket and rang the dime into the cash register. Then he looked expectantly at Jesse.

"What?" Jesse asked.

"Chocolate or strawberry?" Boone hissed in a sloppy whisper.

"Oh! Um. Strawberry."

The store owner nodded. "And another chocolate for you, Boone?"

"I reckon I'll try a strawberry this time, too."

The store owner chuckled. "Glad I'm not your pa. You'd eat me out of house and home."

He took Boone's dish and disappeared into a back room.

Boone wiped his mouth on his shirt sleeve. "I notice the rain's stopped," he said, jerking a chin at the shop window.

"It feels like it's been raining ever since I left Kansas."

"Probably has."

Jesse looked askance at Boone, wondering at that remark. "So," he said after a minute. "Dragons like ice cream?"

Boone shrugged. "I don't know. I never met another dragon, not since my mama disappeared."

Jesse swallowed hard. He didn't know why, but he felt like he could talk to Boone. "My ma is dead," he mumbled.

Boone's cheerful smile fled into a frown. "Gee, I'm awful sorry to hear that. How long ago?"

"About four months. Her baby was born too soon."

"I don't remember much of my mama. I was just a little bitty thing when the evil mage she served was defeated in a war and she took off," Boone said.

Jesse felt his jaw drop. "What?"

Just then, the store owner came back with their ice cream.

Boone's expression brightened immediately, like the sun coming out from behind the clouds. He set to with a vengeance, shoveling ice cream into his mouth so fast Jesse was sure it would freeze his brain. Jesse forgot about his own dish of ice cream as he watched Boone eat.

The store owner chuckled. "No wonder you want to find your own mining claim. You need a heap of gold to satisfy that sweet tooth."

Boone finished the ice cream and picked up the bowl, licking it clean. He came up for air and noticed Jesse's dish, untouched.

"You gonna eat that?" he asked.

Jesse's lips quirked into a ghost of a smile. He slid his dish over to Boone. It was gone in thirty seconds flat.

A woman came in the store and the shopkeeper moved away to help her, still shaking his head at Boone.

Jesse leaned toward Boone. "Dragons sure are crazy about ice cream," he whispered.

Boone cleaned his face with the other sleeve. "Crazy's a strong word."

"You should watch yourself in the mirror next time you eat."

Boone's eyes brightened. "Good idea! A scientific experiment. This calls for more ice cream."

A low, gravelly voice came from behind them. "I think you've had enough, Boone."

Boone's face fell. "Colorow," he whispered conspiratorially to Jesse before swinging around.

The Indian dressed like a Texas Ranger stood behind them, arms crossed over his chest, chiseled face stern. Jesse wondered if his face had any other expression.

"I thought we were supposed to meet back in the street as soon as you were finished," Colorow said.

Boone squirmed on the bar stool. "I got a little distracted."

"So I see." Colorow turned his attention to Jesse. Jesse felt like a bug under a magnifying glass. "You, young man. What's your name?"

Even though he couldn't think of anything he'd done wrong, Jesse found himself wondering if he was about to be arrested. "J...Jesse. Jesse Owens, sir."

"I saw you on the train coming into town. Just moved here, or back from vacation?"

"Just moved here, sir."

Colorow frowned. "Have you ever been to Silver Valley before?"

"N...no, sir. My brother has lived here for a couple of years, though."

"Is that so?" He seemed to lose interest in Jesse. "Come along, Boone. We have work to do." He turned and strode toward the door.

Boone rolled his eyes at Jesse, gave an apologetic smile, and dumped a handful of coins on the counter. "I'm sure we'll bump into each other again soon, Jesse."

Just before Boone sidled out the door after Colorow, Jesse remembered something. "I'm invited to supper at Mrs. Matthews," he called suddenly.

Boone stopped. "Oh, yeah?"

"Ain't you staying there?"

"Yeah. I am. How'd you know?"

Jesse didn't want to admit to spying on Boone earlier, so he ignored the question. "So, I'll see you at supper?" he asked.

Boone smiled. "Sure, kid. See you there."

Chapter 9
Hair in the Butter

Jesse decided to swing by home to let Pa know he wouldn't be there for supper. Pa was pleased Jesse had made a new friend and fended off Jesse's apologies with assurances that Sam and Mary would take care of him.

When Jesse got back to the Matthews' house, Mrs. Matthews and Eliza were nearly finished making supper. Mrs. Matthews handed Jesse a big stack of china plates so he could set the oak table in the dining room. When she told him that not only were Boone and Mr. Colorow boarding there, but Miss Dalton as well, Jesse nearly dropped the china. At least Allan should behave cordially, with all those adults present.

Jesse was nearly finished setting the table when Allan appeared in the doorway. He had obviously just come from the kitchen and was still drying his hands on a towel. "You got a death wish or something, kid?" he said. "Stop hanging around my sister!"

Jesse set down the last plate and squared his shoulders. This was the moment he'd dreaded. "She invited me," he said.

"Well, you should have said no."

"She's the only kid in town who's been nice to me. I ain't about to say no!"

Allan's hands knotted in the towel. He took a step into the room. "I'm warnin' you—"

"Supper time!" Mrs. Matthews boomed from behind Allan. She stood at the bottom of the stairs with a large platter of roast beef. "Supper!"

"This ain't over!" Allan hissed before he turned and ducked back into the kitchen.

Jesse felt the blood rush into his face. Allan didn't have any right to tell him he couldn't be friends with Eliza. From what Eliza had said earlier, Jesse knew she resented her brother's meddling. Allan should let his sister choose her own friends.

A few moments later, when Eliza entered the room, Jesse wasn't sure they were still friends after all. Eliza hardly looked at him and sat on the opposite end of the table. Jesse wondered if Allan had given her a lecture as well, maybe even threatened her, and he felt a new bubble of anger burst inside him. It didn't help his mood when a crack of lightning outside announced a return to the stormy weather.

Jesse's anger subsided a little when Boone showed up behind Colorow.

"Mrs. Matthews puts on the best spread I ever seen!" Boone said appreciatively as he surveyed the dishes Mrs. Matthews kept carting out from the kitchen.

"It'll be a wonder if you don't go home weighing at least a ton more than when we arrived," Colorow grumbled. "Especially after your little 'snack' this afternoon."

Boone patted his stomach and grinned at Jesse. "I got a hollow leg."

Jesse eyed the platter of beef, the pile of steaming potatoes, fresh rolls, and gravy. "Me too," he said.

Allan sat next to Eliza, with Boone and Colorow on the right side of the table, and Jesse at the end. Miss Dalton came in after everyone else, and they all stood up until she was seated on the left beside Allan. She seemed a little flustered, her hands often fiddling with the lace at her throat, but she smiled at Jesse.

"Nice to see you here, Mr. Owens," she said.

Mrs. Matthews bustled in with a tray of roasted carrots just as the storm broke outside. It rained hard. Whipped by the wind, the drops crashed loudly against the windows and roof, making it hard to hear Mrs. Matthews as she bowed her head to offer grace before they started the meal.

As he dished potatoes onto his plate, Jesse watched Eliza from the corner of his eye. She didn't look up enough to see him, but simply took a carrot or two and passed the plate on to her mother.

"I hope this weather clears up before the picnic next Sunday," Mrs. Matthews remarked, pitching her voice loud enough to carry over the pounding rain. "It must be the wettest fall we've had in a decade!"

When she made that remark, Mr. Colorow looked up and peered at Jesse for some reason. Jesse felt his cheeks grow hot under the scrutiny.

"Please pass the butter," he mumbled, trying not to look at Mr. Colorow.

Allan nearly shoved it into his lap.

Mrs. Matthews wiped the corners of her mouth with a napkin. "So, Jesse, what are some of the things you enjoy?"

Jesse looked at Mrs. Matthews. His mind was completely blank.

"Baseball?" Allan asked. He took a big bite of beef and chewed with emphasis.

"I…" Jesse cleared his throat. "I like to play Ring Taw with marbles every so often. And Pa says I'm good with horses."

"That'll come in handy with the ice ponies," Boone said.

Jesse gave him a curious look, but he was distracted from asking Boone what he meant when Miss Dalton gave a sudden cry and leaped back from the table. Gravy dribbled down the front of her dress and spilled from a dropped spoon at the edge of her plate.

"Oh, I'm terribly sorry," she said, wiping at her dress with a napkin.

Mrs. Matthews bustled over, grabbing Allan's napkin to sop up the spill. "Not to worry, dear, not to worry."

Miss Dalton backed toward the doorway, her face red. "I'll just...just go change. I'll only be a moment."

The men all struggled to stand as she left the room. Mr. Colorow watched her go like a mountain lion watches its prey just before it springs.

Boone hardly seemed to notice anything amiss as he shoveled potatoes into his mouth. "I don't take much of a shine to horses myself," he said around a mouthful.

Jesse was quickly losing his appetite. "We had to sell our livestock to move here. Didn't even keep Chip, our big draft horse."

"There ain't much use in farming these parts," Allan said with a sneer. "The growing season's too short."

Jesse nodded at the carrots. "Then where do you get your fresh vegetables?"

Mrs. Matthews came back to her seat. She was flushed and seemed ruffled by the incident with Miss Dalton. "We can grow a few things, especially those that grow fast and keep through the winter, like carrots and peas. Some of our other foodstuff is brought in on the train before the snow gets too deep. Not many people stay here all year round anyway. The place is more or less deserted after the first snowfall."

"Which could be any time now," Allan said. "I expect your pa will want to clear out, go down to Pueblo or someplace until next spring when the mines open again."

"Do you stay here all winter?"

Jesse and Allan stared steadily at each other like a couple of bantam roosters, taking each other's measure.

"Yes," Allan said finally. "By ourselves, mostly."

Miss Dalton reappeared in the doorway, smoothing the front of the gray dress she'd worn at school a couple of days before. She held a dark cape and a pair of gloves in one hand and an umbrella in the other. "Jesse," she said, sounding slightly out of breath. "Are you about finished? I'd like to walk home with you and speak to your father for a few minutes."

Mrs. Matthews leaped from her seat. "But, Miss Dalton, you haven't finished your supper, and you can't go out in this weather. You'll ruin your petticoats in the mud."

Miss Dalton seemed more sure of herself than she had earlier. She brandished the umbrella at Mrs. Matthews. "I don't mind the weather, Mrs. Matthews. Thank you for the supreme meal. It was a delight, as always. Jesse, are you ready?"

Jesse pushed his plate away and scrambled to his feet. "Thanks, Mrs. Matthews," he said. "And Eliza."

They all turned to look at Eliza. She had the ruined side of her face turned away from them and kept her eyes on the floor.

"Eliza?" Mrs. Matthews prompted.

"Thank you for coming, Jesse," she mumbled without moving.

Mrs. Matthews cleared her throat. "Jesse is leaving."

Eliza ducked her head further and pursed her lips closed.

Mrs. Matthews frowned briefly at her daughter before turning to Jesse and replacing the frown with an awkward smile. "You come back soon, Jesse. You're welcome any time."

Allan glared at Jesse behind Mrs. Matthews' back. Eliza still didn't look up. Watching them, Jesse didn't exactly feel welcome to return. At least Boone grinned and waved a fork in the air. His mouth was too full to speak.

The storm had mellowed to a wretched drizzle as Jesse walked home with Miss Dalton under the shelter of her umbrella. It was nearly dark, but light spilled from the houses lining the road.

"Was Eliza able to help you with your reading this afternoon?" Miss Dalton asked.

Jesse shrugged and watched mud splash up onto his boots. He didn't want to talk about Eliza.

"It's hard to make friends in a new place, isn't it?" Miss Dalton finally said. "I've been here for a few months, but I still feel like a stranger sometimes."

The silence stretched between them, heavy as the mud underfoot.

Finally, Miss Dalton spoke again, "What was your home like—in Kansas, wasn't it?"

Jesse swallowed. "Randolph, Kansas."

"Randolph? That sounds familiar. I think I read about that town recently in the newspaper."

Before she could associate his hometown with the storms that had beset the region in the spring, Jesse hastened to add, "We had a farm there. Not much, really. But it was dryer than here. You could see the land for miles around."

"The sunsets must have been beautiful."

"I guess."

"You had friends there, I suppose."

Jesse thought of his friends back home. Harry had probably won everybody's marbles by now without Jesse there to give him competition. "I probably won't ever see them again," he said.

"You never know," Miss Dalton said. "You could always write them a letter." Seeing the look of panic he shot her, she added, "I'll help you, if you'd like."

Jesse hesitated. "Maybe."

They came into the yard of Jesse's cabin. He and Pa had spent the evening yesterday chinking up holes, and not much light leaked through anymore. It looked lonely, with only a little light coming through the window of the front room to ward off the night.

"I forgot. Pa was going to Sam's for supper," Jesse said, suddenly remembering.

"Oh?" Miss Dalton said. She stopped at the bottom step in front of the cabin.

"Maybe you could come back tomorrow," Jesse said.

But just then, the door swung open, and Pa stood framed in the weak light from a gas lamp sitting on the table.

"Jesse?" he asked. "Who's out here with…Miss Dalton!" He smoothed back his hair and hastily tucked in his shirt.

"I don't mean to disturb you, Mr. Owens."

"Not at all, not at all. Won't you come in and have a seat?"

"That's very good of you."

They all moved into the tiny front room of the cabin. Miss Dalton left her umbrella near the door, and Pa helped her off with her cape. He indicated that Miss Dalton should take the rocker, and he and Jesse pulled stools up nearby.

"I won't take much of your time," Miss Dalton began. She folded her gloved hands neatly in her lap. "It's just that I have a small concern about Jesse's schooling. He seems behind in his reading level compared to the other children his age."

Pa frowned. "Jesse's been through a lot recently, Miss Dalton. I expect it's showing up in his schoolwork."

"Yes, well, I had hoped to secure a tutor for him, but that arrangement has fallen through."

Jesse's stomach dropped into his toes. Eliza must have told Miss Dalton she would no longer help Jesse with his reading.

"As such, I wondered if you would allow Jesse to spend some extra time with me after school hours."

"Why, that would be right generous of you, Miss Dalton. I'm sure he would catch up in no time with that extra help."

"I hope so." She stood up, and Pa and Jesse followed suit. "He's a bright boy, and he works hard in class. I'm pleased to have him as a pupil."

"Very kind," Pa said. He slapped a hand on Jesse's shoulder. Jesse felt like he would crumble under the weight. "I think this move has been good for him. He'll catch up in no time."

Pa moved to help Miss Dalton back on with her cape. "I can't have you walking back home by yourself in the dark, Miss Dalton," he said.

"I don't mind. It isn't far."

"No, no. I'll escort you back."

"I couldn't impose, Mr. Owens."

"A lady such as yourself shouldn't be out alone after dark."

Miss Dalton blushed. "Well, if you insist."

Pa opened the door for her. She left the cabin first, and Pa turned back to Jesse before following her out.

"Tomorrow's a school day," he said. "Best get right to bed."

As the door closed behind them, Jesse shuffled into the back room. He plopped down on the edge of Pa's bed and watched rain slide down the window in rivulets. He felt miserable. Just when it had seemed everything would turn out okay, Allan had to go and ruin the only friendship Jesse had found in this awful place.

He knelt on the floor and pried up the loose floorboard. Reaching into the hole, he pulled out the bottle holding dirt from Ma's grave. He wished she were here. Her smile and a hug would have made everything all right again.

Boone went into their room first. Colorow followed and closed the door, leaning back against it and glowering at Boone.

"Are you ever going to learn to control that mouth of yours?" he asked.

Boone blinked at him with wide eyes. "What?"

"That remark you made at dinner. About the ice ponies."

"Oh! I guess folks here would be unfamiliar with ice ponies, but I still don't—"

"The schoolteacher, Miss Dalton. She had her little accident right after you said that. Why?"

"I don't know. She's clumsy?"

"She knows something. I'm sure of it." He moved to the desk and started riffling through papers. "And you need to stop hinting in public that this boy controls the weather."

Boone plopped down on his bed and started pulling off his boots. "Well, he's the thundermage, ain't he?"

"I suspect so, but we don't want everyone else to know that."

Colorow found the paper he was looking for and chucked it across the room. It sailed through the air and landed neatly in Boone's lap. "Take a look at that."

Boone peered at the swirls and squiggles on the paper. He couldn't make head or tails of it. "What is it?"

"A weather report from that big storm system last spring. Guess where it started."

"I know you ain't gonna say Randolph, Kansas."

"Yes. The same place that boy told you he was from." Colorow's mouth twisted into a wry frown. "When you weren't supposed to be talking to him."

Boone swallowed. "You think he's causing the mining accidents?"

"I don't know. It doesn't seem typical for a thundermage."

"Who else could it be?"

"Believe me, there are plenty of possibilities in this town."

"Like who?"

"That teacher, for one."

"You suspect her? But she smells so nice, like roses."

"Roses have thorns, Boone. You were very young when the Katsina last dealt with a skinwalker. You don't remember what it's like."

"All I know is that skinwalkers served Orendos. They're pure evil."

"They were his most valuable servants," Colorow said. "They are very powerful."

"But the Katsina can defeat them."

"Working together, maybe. If one Katsina faced a skinwalker alone, I'm not sure which would win. Skinwalkers have a magic of their own, a dark magic that walked the world even before dragons ruled. But a skinwalker is most dangerous because it can pose as anyone."

Boone frowned. "How does it do that?"

"I see your education has been neglected in more than just glyphs."

Boone's face flushed with embarrassment, even though he tried to hide it.

"A skinwalker steals something from its victim," Colorow continued. "It could be a lock of hair, a fingernail, or in your case, a dragon scale. This allows the skinwalker to assume the identity of that person."

"Even a mage?" Boone asked.

"Especially a mage," Colorow said. "A skinwalker would be drawn to a mage's power. It would covet that power for its own."

"And what happens to the fellow missing a scale?" Boone asked, not sure he wanted to know the answer.

"The skinwalker not only steals a part of its victim, it steals their very essence, their soul. No one can survive without a soul."

"They die?"

"Yes. That is why you must be on your guard. The skinwalker could be anyone, even this boy."

Boone didn't want it to be Jesse. "I don't reckon the kid is evil like that. He just don't seem too keen on being here. Maybe he's causing the accidents so his pa will take him home to Kansas."

"I doubt it's that simple, not when a shard of the Wité Pot is hidden somewhere nearby."

"Right." Boone tasted bile at the reminder. "The thing I'm supposed to destroy."

"You are the only surviving dragon we know about. Your mother made the Wité Pot for Orendos to trap the Katsina and hold them captive to his will. When we were finally able to defeat Orendos, we could only shatter the pot and hide the shards, not destroy it. It is fitting you should finish the job."

The conversation had turned more uncomfortable than Boone liked. He changed the subject.

"How do you know them mining accidents ain't just accidents, like the sheriff said?"

Colorow rubbed a hand across his eyes, as if he were tired. "A Katsina was assigned to live in this valley," he said. "He was here to protect the Wité shard, keep it safe. I haven't been able to find him. Something happened."

"Foul play?"

"Foul play. And I cannot think of anything aside from Orendos himself that could threaten a Katsina more than a skinwalker."

Boone shivered as a sudden draft from the window brushed against his arms. He thought he could smell gunpowder.

Colorow's lips thinned into a smile, but it was without humor. "We're playing a dangerous game, Boone Evans. But I have never lost at it before, and I don't intend to do so now."

Chapter 10
Wallowing in Velvet

It was raining. Still. Jesse cursed the day Pa dragged him to such a wet, miserable hole in the ground where he would never see the sun again.

Because of the rain, the children had to stay indoors for recess on Friday. The girls huddled in a circle in one back corner, playing Fly Away, Pigeon. The girl in the middle of the group raised a finger and called out an animal that could fly. The other girls had to follow her lead, but she often tricked them by calling out an animal that could not fly, causing several girls to move their fingers when they shouldn't and forfeit the game. Girlish giggles drifted frequently across the room.

The boys took up the other corner where they had drawn a circle on the floor in chalk to play Ring Taw with marbles made of baked clay, called muddies. Jesse huddled at the edge of the group, ignored by everyone and feeling as miserable as the weather.

"There it goes!" yelled one of the boys as a large shooter muddy, called a taw, hit a muddy inside the circle. The muddy rolled to the edge of the circle, but stopped before it crossed the chalk line.

"Too bad, Zeke," Allan said, grinning across the circle at his opponent. "My turn."

Allan shifted around the edge of the circle and took up a shooting position with his taw. Allan was as good at this game as he was at baseball. He had nearly cleaned out the circle, claiming all the boys' muddies for himself. Zeke was the last opponent.

Jesse fingered the handful of muddies in his pocket. He had been a good Ring Taw player at home in Kansas. When Pa dragged him to Silver Valley, Jesse had brought the best of his collection with him, those that were smooth and weighted just right. Some he had made himself and painted with simple lines and circles. Some he had won from other boys. So far, Jesse hadn't gotten a chance to use them.

Allan placed his hand on the floor, palm facing up with his taw curled inside his index finger, knuckling down and taking aim.

"I hope the rain doesn't spoil the community picnic this Sunday," Miss Dalton said.

Jesse hadn't heard her come up behind him, and he jumped a little.

"Are you and your father planning to attend?" she asked.

Jesse shrugged. The picnic sounded like fun, but only if he had friends to share it with. Right now, his prospects seemed pretty dismal. He glanced over at the girls. He couldn't see Eliza.

Allan flicked the taw forward with his thumb. It rolled into the circle and hit Zeke's taw. The boys cheered loudly.

"That's it!" Allan said with a laugh. "You forfeit the game to me and all your muddies!"

"What?" Zeke shouted, jumping to his feet.

Miss Dalton placed a firm hand on Zeke's shoulder. "You agreed to those rules, Zeke. Now, be a good sport."

Zeke glared at her a moment before stomping off to his desk and sliding into it, arms crossed over his chest.

Allan looked around at the boys while he gathered up his new muddies. "Who's next?" Nobody answered. Most of the boys suddenly found an interest in cleaning their fingernails or polishing their shoes on a pant leg. "Doesn't anybody want to challenge me?" Allan asked.

Jesse was just about to step forward when Miss Dalton moved past him.

"Very well, Allan," she said. "You asked for it."

Allan laughed. "Miss Dalton? Are you joshing me?"

She knelt carefully at the edge of the chalk circle, arranging her skirts modestly. "I would never do that, Allan," she said with a wink.

She held out a handful of marbles. None of them were made of clay. Jesse had heard of glass marbles, made back East in the big cities, but he had never seen any. They were smooth and perfectly round, with surfaces that caught the light of the lamps in the room and glittered like mirrors. Colors danced inside each marble in intricate patterns. Jesse "oohed" and "ahhed" with the other boys. He had never seen anything so fantastic.

A greedy glint caught fire in Allan's eye. "How many muddies...I mean, marbles, in the circle, ma'am?" he asked.

Miss Dalton studied her glass collection. "Let's see. I have five here, plus a taw. How about we do all five?"

Allan's smile spread slowly across his face. "Suits me."

He counted out five of the muddies he had won from the other boys and placed them in a line inside the circle. Miss Dalton did the same with her glass marbles, lining them up perpendicular to the muddies so that all the marbles formed an "X." The glass marbles looked elegant and sophisticated against the muddies, like shiny apples beside moldy potatoes.

"Should we shoot to see who goes first?" Miss Dalton asked.

Allan gestured grandly with one hand. "Ladies go first, of course, ma'am."

Miss Dalton fought a losing battle with a grin. "All right, Allan."

She crouched next to a line drawn a handspan outside the circle, called the offing, from which the first shot with the taw was always taken. Curling her large glass shooter inside her index finger and laying her hand palm up on the floor beside the offing, she knuckled down and flicked the shooter with her thumb to send it spinning into the circle. It bumped a muddy and stopped, sticking to the spot. The muddy rolled forward, crossing the chalk line to exit the circle.

"That's one," she said brightly, picking up the muddy.

Allan's face had lost a little of its eagerness. Miss Dalton shifted around on the floor to get at her taw. The group of boys moved around her as if they were all involved in some elaborate dance without music. The girls noticed that something unusual was happening. They stopped their game and came over to watch.

It took Miss Dalton no more than a minute to shoot all the muddies and glass marbles out of the circle. The children were silent as they watched Miss Dalton soundly defeat Allan. Never once did she miss a target, or fail to hit it outside the circle. Allan didn't get a chance to shoot his taw at all.

When it was over, she said cheerfully, "Better luck next time, Allan."

No one seemed to move or breathe. Allan's mouth hung open in shock as he stared at her, reflecting the expression on many of the children's faces. Jesse knew his chance to play would soon be gone.

Leaping forward, he said breathlessly, "I'll play you a round, Miss Dalton."

Miss Dalton looked up in surprise. She picked up the watch pinned to her bodice. "I suppose we have a little time before recess is over."

Jesse crouched across the circle from her, taking Allan's place. He could feel Allan's eyes on his back, boring holes through his spine. Carefully, Jesse pulled his muddies out of his pocket, counting out five and placing them precisely in a row inside the circle.

"Those are lovely, Jesse," Miss Dalton said. "Did you paint them yourself?"

"Some of them," Jesse mumbled.

"I will cherish them in my collection," Miss Dalton said with a twinkle in her eye.

She lined up her marbles perpendicular to his.

"I won the last game, so you're welcome to shoot first," Miss Dalton said.

Jesse inclined his head. "As Allan said, ladies first."

"Are you sure? You saw what I did the last time."

"I saw." Jesse studied the placement of his muddies. "And I'm sure."

Miss Dalton shook her head and crouched near the offing, curling her finger around her shooter and flicking it into the circle. It whizzed forward, hitting one of Jesse's muddies and sending it out of the circle.

Miss Dalton's smile was apologetic. "That's one," she said.

Jesse felt his insides tighten. Would she beat him as soundly as she had beaten Allan? He studied the placement of the marbles, analyzing the resting place of her taw and the angles she might take to hit his muddies. There were too many possibilities.

Miss Dalton picked up her taw where it had stopped on the last shoot and knuckled down, taking aim. She flicked the taw hard with her thumb. It rolled forward, but the angle was slightly off. It glanced off the side of a muddy, pushing it forward, but not far enough to exit the circle. Miss Dalton's taw continued moving until it rolled out of the circle and stopped near a boy's toe. There was a collective sigh of disappointment.

Miss Dalton frowned. "How did that happen?" she said.

Jesse didn't know, but he was eager to take advantage of her mistake. "My turn."

Moving around the outer rim of the circle to the offing, Jesse forced the boys watching to make room for him. He took his time, positioning his shooting hand carefully and visually lining up the taw with his target. When he felt ready, he pushed the taw forward with his thumb, sending it into a spin into the circle. He held his breath with the rest of the crowd as he watched the taw roll away.

It tapped a muddy with just the right amount of force, sticking the taw in place and sending the muddy out of the circle on the other side. The shot left Jesse's taw close to the center of the circle, near the other marbles. After that, it was an easy matter to send the rest of the marbles out of the circle.

Miss Dalton laughed as Jesse scooped up her last glass marble. "Well, I do declare, Jesse Owens! I believe you have whipped me fair and square."

One of the children started clapping, and soon they were all clapping. Jesse looked up in amazement at the smiles and friendly expressions around him.

Miss Dalton stood and brushed off her skirts. "Children, please be seated. It's about time we resumed our studies."

As Jesse picked up his taw, he caught several admiring glances from the other boys. He knew he would have more takers at Ring Taw in the near future. His collection was about to grow by leaps and bounds.

Jesse stood up and helped some of the other boys move the desks back into place over the chalked circle. As he did so, he caught Eliza's eye from her seat in the far corner. He grinned at her, holding up his handful of marbles. But she turned away from him with a haughty expression and buried her nose in her reader.

Jesse felt a crushing disappointment that turned to anger like the flash of a wildfire. He didn't need her friendship. She was just a freakish girl nobody liked anyway. She hadn't done him any favors. After all, he was doing all right at making his own friends in Silver Valley. He'd show her. Soon, he'd be the most popular boy in class.

Chapter 11
Catching a Weasel Asleep

Boone tossed the dingy cap on his bed, not caring whether it broke the lamp fastened to the front. He grabbed his Stetson from the hat stand and jammed it low onto his head in defiance.

"I don't see why I have to be the one to go down into that mine."

Colorow didn't look up from where he faced the window, working at the desk with his back to Boone. "What did you find out?"

"That I hate mining." He stomped to the washbasin, poured water into it from the delicate pitcher nearby, and scrubbed vigorously at his arms with lye soap. "It's gonna take me a year to get all this dirt off." He wished he could fly high into the air and let off some steam, maybe take a swim in that lake near the Bellawest, but Colorow had forbidden him to transform ever since Jesse had seen him as a dragon last Sunday.

"I'll have Mrs. Matthews draw you a bath," Colorow said. He set down his pen and swung around to give Boone his full attention. "So, what did you find out?"

Boone snorted. "Nothing worth all this muck. Everybody knows who Madge is, but nobody's seen her for more than a fortnight. They all repeated rumors about the widowmaker. Nobody I talked to has seen her for hisself."

"Did you get any names of those who actually saw her?"

"One. A Bill something-or-another. It was back last summer away up in the Sabina mine."

"Sabina." Colorow swung back around and resumed scratching at a paper with his pen. "Did they say exactly when he saw her?"

"No. They just said last summer."

"I can probably get that information from the sheriff."

"Sure you can. If you pry it out of his mouth with a crowbar."

Colorow glanced up, chuckling softly. "You might be on to something."

Boone wasn't in the mood to laugh at his own joke. He dried his hands on a nearby towel and frowned when he left dark streaks on the white fabric.

"Come here," Colorow said.

Boone sauntered up behind him and looked at the large sheet of paper Colorow held out. "What's that?"

"This is a map." He pointed to several circle shapes. "These mark where the accidents we know of have occurred. I've written the dates next to each one. Do you see a pattern?"

"I'm even worse at human stuff than dragon glyphs."

Colorow gave an exaggerated sigh. "They start here, in the mine furthest from Silver Valley. They move slowly closer. I think the Ulay might be next."

"Great. I'll probably be on my shift when the whole mountain collapses on my head."

"It just means you've got to be on your toes."

Boone noticed several symbols drawn in the upper right corner of the map. "Are those dragon glyphs?"

"Yes, but they're not a magic spell. They're just some notes I made about the Wité Pot."

Boone pointed to one of the glyphs. It was an oblong circle with two dots in the middle. "That one looks familiar."

Colorow cocked an eyebrow. "Don't tell me you've been studying."

Boone's face reddened. "No. I ain't had time to study, what with all the…" He suddenly remembered and snapped his fingers. "That's it! I saw it down in the tunnels today, chiseled on one of them walls. A petro-what-cha-ma-call-it from a long time ago. I remember because I thought it looked like a pig nose."

Colorow was on his feet so fast, he knocked the chair over. "Show me."

"What? I just got off my shift. What do I tell the foreman when I show up again?"

Grabbing his coat off the rack, Colorow shoved his arms into it and briskly rolled up his map. "The foreman doesn't need to know we're there."

"So, we're gonna just waltz in and out of a commercial mine in broad daylight with nobody the wiser?"

Colorow yanked the door open and strode out. "Yes."

Boone growled and made a grab for the cap with the light. He raced out the door after Colorow. "Wait up! What about my bath?"

Slipping past the humans to get into the Ulay was the easy part. Finding where Boone had seen the glyph was the hard part.

Boone and Colorow wandered the tunnels for the remainder of the day. When they came upon workers, or heard them coming, Colorow would trace a symbol in the air, and they would duck into a side passage or an alcove with nobody the wiser. Once, Colorow's magic allowed

111

them to stand perfectly still to one side of a tunnel while two miners walked past with shovels, jabbering away and never noticing them.

It was cold and dark in the tunnels. The light on Boone's hat seemed feeble and weak compared with the darkness pressing in all around them. Colorow had swiped a lantern from the entrance, but even that wasn't enough to chase away the gloom. Boone tried not to brush up against the dirty walls or the beams holding up the roof, but it felt like the very air was full of grit, infusing Boone's lungs with each breath and seeping into his skin until he was sure he would never be rid of it.

Colorow grew more and more impatient with each wrong turn Boone took.

They hadn't seen another worker for at least an hour when Boone finally realized they were close to the glyph. "I think it's just around that bend ahead," he said.

"That's what you said the last time," Colorow snapped.

"This time, I'm sure...well, pretty sure. The foreman was in a hurry to get us to the mucking site and we took a shortcut. The miners hardly never go this way otherwise."

It soon became obvious they were no longer in a man-made tunnel, but a natural cave. The walls were rougher, and there were no more wooden beams like giant animal ribs framing the tunnel. Boone nearly cracked his head on a

112

ceiling that got lower and lower. Finally, they came to a cleft in the rock just wide enough for a man to squeeze through sideways.

"Here it is!" Boone said. "It's just past this crack. Not far."

"About time." Colorow brushed past Boone and took off his gun, handing it to Boone.

After Colorow shimmied through, he reached back for the gun. Then Boone blew out his breath and held it to make himself as thin as he could while he squeezed into the cleft. The passage was narrow, making him grateful for the heavy mining coveralls he wore. As soon as he reached the chamber beyond, he had an uneasy feeling, like an itch in the middle of his back that he couldn't quite reach.

The chamber wasn't large, maybe ten paces across and fifteen long. It was an odd shape, with dark corners Boone had no desire to investigate. The air was stale and smelled of damp earth. A larger opening on the far side led to the mucking site Boone had visited earlier in the day. The metallic ring of shovels on stone and the shouting of men were absent now. Boone thought it must be near quitting time.

"The glyph is over there," he said, pointing to the low ceiling on the right. The aged chiseling of petroglyphs long forgotten seemed to jump out of the stone as Colorow drew near and held his lantern light up to them. He set down his gun and studied the petroglyphs for several long minutes.

Boone did his best to make out the meaning of the glyphs. They were supposed to be the language of the dragons, but he had a difficult time understanding what they meant. The Katsina had tried to teach him—hoping he would be able to make magical items for them, no doubt. But so far, he had proven to be a slow study.

There was a rough figure of a man without a head. The left hand was shaped funny, with a circle and curved lines above it. The right arm was stretched straight out, with lines coming out of it as if falling off the arm. Higher on the panel was an upside-down half circle with a dot inside. The pig-nose shape was placed down and to the right of the headless man, a rough circle with two smaller circles inside and a bunch of smaller dots. Over it all, two arrows met head on.

So, if Boone figured right, the glyphs said a man would embrace flying pigs that would betray him by cutting off his head when the moon was half full.

"That's the glyph for Orendos," Colorow said. He pointed to the headless man. "He was punished for practicing forbidden magic, which is why he has no head. The shape you took for a pig nose," Colorow spared Boone a scathing glance, "refers to the Wité Pot itself. The circles inside mean looking or seeking. The little dots represent power trapped inside the larger circle. Then this," he pointed to the upside-down half circle, "means something hidden. The shard, I'm sure."

"I knew that," Boone said with what he hoped was a confident nod.

Colorow held his lantern higher and peered at the petroglyphs. "So it tells us what we already know, that there is a shard of the Wité Pot hidden nearby, but it doesn't say exactly where."

The sound of a hammer rang suddenly through the chamber, three quick taps that echoed and bounced off the rock.

Boone looked over at the exit. "Have we been here all night? Are they starting the morning shift already?"

The three taps were repeated, like the knell of doom.

"That's no miner," Colorow said. His face looked grim. But then, it always did. "That's a tommyknocker. Stay here."

Colorow left the chamber in four long strides, exiting toward the mucking site.

Boone's stomach tied itself into knots. Tommyknockers were small creatures that lived in the bowels of the earth. They were rarely seen, especially by humans, but they gave warning to miners when a disaster was imminent. There was a rumor in the Veiled Canyon that one lived in hidden caves behind the Central Kiva.

Colorow's voice came back from the mucking site, faint with distance. "I don't see him. You can…"

He didn't finish. A deep rumble came from the bowels of the earth, and the ground beneath Boone's feet trembled as if it feared what was coming.

"Boone!" Colorow yelled. "Get down!"

Boone dove for the ground, covering his head with his arms. The ground bucked and heaved. Rocks and dirt fell on him, thumping him in tender places. He wished he had the space in this chamber to transform. His dragon scales would have protected him from the worst of it. As it was, he felt like a kitten in a hailstorm.

It was over in a moment.

When he was sure the ground would hold him upright again, Boone climbed unsteadily to his feet. The air was full of dust. He coughed, trying to clear it from his lungs. Now he really never would get clean again.

As the dust settled, he took stock of his situation. The chamber remained intact, but a large pile of rubble blocked the exit to the mucking site, where Colorow had gone. Boone spun. One of the slabs at the cleft where they'd entered had shifted, making the opening too small for him to get out.

He waved dust away from his face and coughed, a sinking feeling in the pit of his belly. He was alone. And he was trapped.

Chapter 12
Between a Rock and a Hard Place

Jesse decided to go fishing after school. He was surprised to find Pa home when he arrived. Pa had gotten off work early and asked to join Jesse. Hesitantly, Jesse agreed. They gathered their gear and walked the half mile up the road to Crystal Lake.

Pa slung an arm casually across Jesse's shoulders. "Your ma would have loved this place," he said, looking around at the trees crowding the road. "She loved growing things."

"Too bad she never got to see it," Jesse mumbled.

Pa looked down at Jesse. "That is too bad. But we're here, ain't we? And things have been better here."

Meaning, Jesse knew, that no chickens had been mysteriously frozen and no whirlwinds had appeared out of nowhere to carry off the laundry.

"That teacher of yours," Pa began slowly.

"Miss Dalton?"

"Do you like her?"

Jesse shrugged. "Sure, I guess. I mean, I won five glass marbles from her today."

Pa laughed with surprise. "She played you at Ring Taw?"

Jesse felt a smile tug at the corners of his mouth. "Yeah."

"Then she deserved what she got. She should have known better than to go up against the best Ring Taw player in ten counties." He gave Jesse's shoulders a squeeze.

Jesse blushed. "It wasn't easy, beating her. She's good."

"Is she now?"

They reached the lake. It stretched before them, the water dark as it reflected the clouds brooding above it. At least it wasn't raining, Jesse thought.

They set their lines and waited on the fish as the afternoon stretched into evening. They caught five good-sized trout. Jesse cleaned them with the knife he kept in a sheath at his waist. Pa suggested they ask Mary to fry them up for supper.

Mary made a meal out of it, with fresh cornbread and roasted potatoes alongside green string beans. Jesse felt himself relax in the rocking chair of Sam's front room as he took in the smells of fried fish and baked cornbread.

Sam and Mary kept a small clapboard house a few streets down from Pa and Jesse with white-washed walls and a kitchen separate from the front room. Mary's homey touches were evident everywhere, from the afghan draped over the rocking chair to the lacy curtains at the windows and embroidery hung on the walls.

Sam interrupted Jesse's tranquility by shoving a stack of plates into his middle. "Here you go, Sprout. Set the table, would ya?"

Jesse groaned and moved sluggishly to obey, pulling himself out of the comfortable chair and heading for the kitchen. Before he could get there, he heard Mary's cry of dismay.

"What's wrong, love?" Sam asked, ducking into the kitchen with a concerned expression.

He backed out a moment later, Mary following him and shaking an empty crock in his face. "The very last drop of honey, Sam? Really?"

Sam flushed as he backed up against a wall. "You can't eat biscuits without honey, love."

Mary sighed heavily. "And just what am I supposed to serve with the cornbread tonight?"

Pa took the stem of his pipe out of his mouth and knocked the ashes into a nearby tray. "Don't fret, Mary. We got honey. Jesse!"

"Yes, Pa?"

"Run home and fetch our crock of honey for supper."

"Yes, sir." Jesse set the plates back on the sideboard with a wicked grin at Sam.

"Hurry it up," Pa said, "or there won't be nothing left for you to eat when you get back."

That wiped the smile off Jesse's face. He gulped. He was out the door in a flash and running down the road.

Twilight lay heavy on the valley. It would be full dark soon. Lights from the houses he passed flashed with glimpses of the lives behind those doors. He ran through the streets, ignoring the mud splashing up on his pant legs.

The cabin was dark as he raced into the yard and up to the porch. A rumble of thunder announced the intentions of the clouds above. Jesse grabbed the knob of the front door. It was cold in his hand, colder than it should be. It brought him up short. With a sudden feeling of dread, he turned the knob and pushed the door open.

Inside it was even colder—so cold, he could see his breath as he stepped into the front room. He wondered briefly if he should build a fire, but forgot the notion when he saw the inside of the cabin. Ice covered everything, making the surfaces glitter in the dying light of day. Shadows clung to the corners, darkest in the doorway leading to the back room.

Jesse groaned. It was just like the chicken coop back home in Kansas. He had to somehow get rid of all this ice before Pa saw it.

He thought he heard something move in the back bedroom, and the bottom dropped out of his stomach. "Who's there?" he said in a quivering voice. Nobody answered.

He wanted to turn and bolt right back out of the cabin and into the yard, but he gritted his teeth and took a step forward instead.

The floor had a fine mist of frost that crackled under his weight as he moved slowly forward. His eyes were glued on the doorway to the back room. He studied the shadows, trying to make out whoever hid in them.

As Jesse got closer, he thought he could see the outline of a person huddled on the floor just inside the doorway.

"Who's there?" he whispered again.

For several seconds that felt like an eternity, there was no other sound. Then, someone whispered, "Jesse."

Jesse nearly jumped out of his skin. It sounded for all the world like his mother. Was he seeing a ghost?

The figure shifted and unwound, climbing unsteadily to its feet. Jesse could vaguely make out a face.

He swallowed, feeling foolish and angry. "Eliza? What are you doing here?"

She sniffed, and he could tell she'd been crying. "Something awful has happened."

He peered into her face. "What? What's wrong?"

She hiccupped with a suppressed sob, and his anger immediately fled.

"Is it your ma? Allan?"

She shook her head. "No, no. It's…" She struggled to speak around her emotion. "There's been an accident. A mining accident. At the Ulay—" Her words choked off in another sob as she clamped a hand over her mouth, staring at him with eyes swimming in tears.

"Hey there." Jesse moved instinctively toward her, putting out a hand to comfort her.

She gasped and disappeared.

Jesse stared at the shadow where she'd been. Suddenly, he lunged for the sideboard, grabbing a stray candle. The wick burst into flame, light flooding the room. He held the candle up, moving it around to search every corner and hiding place he could think of. He was alone.

Then Eliza's words sank in. An accident. At a mine. He had to tell Pa!

Jesse blew out the candle, turning to run as hard as he could back to Sam's house.

It wasn't until much later that Jesse realized he hadn't used a match to light the candle.

The light of Boone's headlamp seemed to be fading. He didn't know if this was just his imagination, or if the lamp was running out of oil. If it was the latter, he would soon be left in darkness.

He had tried moving the rock debris that blocked the exit, but when the pile shifted ominously, he feared he would cause another cave in that would bury him this time. So, now he sat with his back to a rock wall, Colorow's gun across his lap, staring up at the dragon glyphs chiseled on the opposite ceiling.

Colorow should have gotten him out by now. A Katsina used magic to control the elements—surely Colorow could find a way to get Boone out of the chamber. Unless something had happened to Colorow. Boone shuddered to think of it.

He had always considered the Katsina invincible. But what if this widowmaker had caused the earthquake in order to separate Colorow from Boone? She could have attacked Colorow while Boone was trapped here, unable to help. Colorow said a Katsina and a skinwalker were equally matched in power, but surely the odds would improve with a dragon in the fight.

Boone picked up a rock and chucked it across the cave, where it hit several other rocks and caused a small cascade. If Colorow was in trouble, Boone wanted to help. He cursed himself for not following Colorow out of the chamber before the quake started.

The petroglyphs had returned to their weathered state now that Colorow wasn't nearby to strengthen their magic. The fading light of Boone's headlamp didn't help. But Boone thought he saw a petroglyph that Colorow hadn't translated. He stood up and moved closer to the glyphs, trying to make out the symbol. It was a handspan above the others, somewhat obscured by a crack running through the rock and painted over in a rusty red color that had faded to more of an orange.

He studied it for several moments, then reached up to trace the lines with a finger. This helped him make the connections with the missing parts of the glyph so he was able to figure out the whole pattern. There were three symbols. The first looked like a spiral, the second like three wavy lines, and the third like two circles, one inside the other, located far to the right. What did it mean? And why hadn't Colorow included these glyphs when he translated the petroglyph for Boone? Hadn't Colorow seen them?

Noticing the rolled-up map Colorow had dropped when he left the chamber earlier, Boone stooped to pick it up. He searched around for a bit of charcoal and found some crumbling red sandstone. He studied the petroglyphs, then spread the paper across the rock and rubbed the sandstone over it. The petroglyphs below caused a relief image to appear on the unmarked side of Colorow's map, creating a copy of the dragon glyphs.

Boone's nose caught the whiff of a new smell. He stopped rubbing and became instantly alert. The scent was of frozen dust and the dry leaves of fall mingled with a sulfur-like acidity that stung his nostrils. Magic.

"Colorow?"

Boone slowly circled the chamber, seeking the source of the smell. It seemed to be coming from the slabs of rock where he and Colorow had entered the chamber, now blocked by the shifted rock.

"Colorow?" he called again. His voice cracked as he added, "That you?"

"Don't worry," a voice whispered back. "I'll get you out."

Boone stumbled back a couple of steps. That hadn't been Colorow. It was a girl's voice.

As he watched, the stone seemed to shimmer, as if Boone watched it through a haze of heat. There was a groan, the rock protesting, and the slab began to move. Boone stepped back again.

The opening became just wide enough for a man to fit through, if he was thin enough.

"You must hurry," said the girl's voice from the shadows beyond the opening. "I cannot hold it for long."

Boone swallowed hard. Making sure he had a tight grip on the petroglyph rubbing in one hand and Colorow's rifle in the other, he leaped forward, jamming his body between the slabs and wriggling through as fast as he could. The passage was narrower than it had been before. The rock walls scraped against his skin, tearing his clothes, but he forced his way through, hanging on to the barrel of Colorow's gun as if it were pushing him.

Boone's headlamp picked out a figure in the passage beyond, but it wasn't until he staggered out the other side of the crevice that he could make out details.

A girl stood in the passage beyond the cleft, one hand raised and resting gently against the rock slab that had fallen in the earthquake.

She had black hair braided into two long ropes that hung down her back. Feathers trailed from a thong tied around her brow. She wore a simple buckskin dress fringed at the hem and sleeves. An armband of silver studded with turquoise circled the bicep of her right arm. Her pretty face was knotted in concentration, beads of perspiration on her high forehead. The smell of cold acid got stronger as he approached her. It felt as if his nose hairs were freezing, a sensation he had only felt occasionally when a Katsina worked powerful magic near him. But that was impossible. He didn't see a glyph anywhere, and she wasn't a Katsina. She was just a girl...wasn't she?

Once Boone was free, the girl moved her hand off the rock slab. It fell back into place with a hollow boom that danced away in echoes down the passage. The girl sighed quietly and collapsed in a faint.

Boone grabbed for her reflexively, catching her just before she hit the ground.

"Miss?" Boone said hesitantly. He patted one of her cheeks with a free hand. "Miss?"

He heard a faint shout from some distance down the passage. "It came from over there!"

He looked up, peering into the darkness.

"I see a light!" someone else shouted.

The girl in Boone's arms suddenly opened her eyes. She stared up at him, blinking in confusion.

"Are you okay?" Boone asked.

Another shout seemed closer.

The girl sat up sharply. "Someone is coming," she whispered, staring down the passage with what looked like terror in her eyes.

"I reckon it's a resc—"

Before he could finish, the girl suddenly disappeared. One moment, he felt her weight against his arms, and the next, nothing. He stumbled forward before he could adjust his balance, then turned in a full circle. Her smell was gone too.

The light in the tunnel grew brighter as three miners ran toward him. They huffed and gasped for breath.

"You all right, fella?" one man asked.

Boone took off his hat to run a hand through his bushy hair. "I reckon I'm still in one piece, but we'd best get on out of here. I think I just saw the widowmaker."

The rescuers thoroughly searched the Ulay and pulled out two other men besides Boone. Neither of them was Colorow. The foreman said they were lucky it had happened after regular operation hours, when precious few workers were inside. The damage was minimal, mostly in one area of the mine not used much anyway. In fact, it wasn't even officially part of the Ulay, just an old passage and a cave that connected two areas of the commercial operation. The sheriff said they'd keep looking for survivors.

Boone spent a restless night waiting for Colorow to show up. He never came. By the time his window grew light, Boone was forced to admit that something had gone wrong.

He sat at Colorow's desk, watching the sun tickle the mountaintops to the east of the valley. He felt alone and lost. Had the skinwalker trapped Colorow, just as Boone had been trapped? Was Colorow defeated, or worse, dead? If the widowmaker was the skinwalker, why had she freed Boone? He had too many questions and no answers.

Shifting his arms on the desk, he noticed the stack of papers piled under them. They still smelled like Colorow, a blend of wood smoke and leather tinged with the sharpness of magic.

Boone picked up a couple of the papers. They were covered in human writing and dragon glyphs he couldn't decipher. They reminded Boone of the glyphs he and Colorow had found in the Ulay.

He fetched the rubbings he had made. Spreading the paper out, he examined it. But his brain felt fuzzy, and his eyes seemed packed in sand. He didn't think he could figure out what any of the glyphs meant until he got some sleep.

Chapter 13
Hold On to Your Horses

Jesse slept late Saturday morning. He had stayed up much of the night, waiting with Mary outside the Ulay as Sam and Pa joined the rescue mission. They were able to help a handful of men trapped underground, including Boone. When Pa and Sam were relieved by reinforcements, the foreman of the Bellawest gave them a half day off. Jesse assumed Pa would sleep late too.

But he didn't.

Jesse woke to the sound of a horse stamping and blowing and whinnying outside. Dashing sleep from his eyes, he threw on a pair of overalls and rushed out the door in bare feet.

Pa and Sam were in the yard, holding the lead rope of a beautiful chestnut stallion. They shouted and cussed as the horse fought the lead with all it had.

Jesse ran down the steps.

"Get back, son!" Pa shouted when he saw Jesse.

The horse tried to sunfish, nearly pulling Pa and Sam off their feet.

"What did you do to him?" Jesse demanded angrily.

"Nothing!" Sam protested. "He came this way. Ornery cuss."

"Don't call him that!" Jesse yelled.

"Jesse," Pa said, "fetch a bag of oats from the shed yonder."

Jesse ran to obey, ignoring the dig of the rough ground on his bare feet. He found a feedbag in the shed and a large sack of oats. After filling the feedbag, he had an idea and ran to the house. He grabbed a bowl of apples off the sideboard. When he got back to the yard, he set the food down and picked up an apple in each hand. He inched slowly toward the horse.

"Hey, boy!" he shouted in a cheerful voice, waving the apples and trying to get the horse's attention. "Look what I got here. C'mon, boy. You like apples? That's right. Smell them apples. They're good, ain't they?"

The horse caught sight of Jesse and the apples and didn't jerk away quite so hard. Jesse continued to offer the apples, keeping up a steady dialogue. Slowly, the horse calmed down. As it quit pulling at the lead rope, Jesse moved closer, still talking.

"Careful," Sam said.

The horse rolled its eyes toward Sam and jerked its head.

"Hush up, Sam," Pa said.

Jesse ignored them, keeping his eyes on the horse as he crept ever nearer with the apples. He got close enough that he could feel the horse's hot breath on his skin. He shifted his grip on one of the apples so it sat on the palm of his hand and moved it slowly toward the horse's nose.

"C'mon, boy," he said softly. "You know you want it. Go ahead. It won't hurt you."

The horse snorted in Jesse's face and then, as if taking advantage of the distraction, it snatched at the apple with its teeth, nearly taking Jesse's hand off in the process.

Jesse chuckled and held out the other apple. The horse made short work of that one, too.

"Hold the lead, Sam," Pa said.

He moved carefully to where Jesse had dropped the oats and the other apples. When he returned, he handed Jesse another apple. Jesse held it out for the horse to eat and stroked its sweaty shoulder with his other hand.

"That's right," Jesse said. "You're a good boy, ain't you?"

Pa slipped the feedbag over the horse's head, and soon the horse was munching contentedly on oats. Jesse continued to stroke its sides as it ate while Sam tied the lead to a hitching post in the yard.

Tipping his hat back to wipe the sweat from his brow, Pa said, "I can see why the miner woman who sold me this horse was so keen to let him go at a bargain price."

"You mean," Jesse said, "he's ours?"

"I know you've missed Chip something fierce, son. I wanted to make it up to you, since things have gone so well here in our new home."

Jesse's stomach did a flip-flop. He hadn't told Pa about the ice that had been all over the cabin last night. When they'd returned from the mining rescue, everything was back to normal.

"But," Pa continued, "this horse ain't no mild-mannered Chip. I've half a mind to return him after that display."

"No!" Jesse said. "I want to keep him."

Sam leaned against the hitching post and wiped sweat from his face. "You got a hankering for trouble, Sprout?"

"He ain't trouble. Just because he don't like *you*."

"Jesse," Pa said, "I don't see what we're gonna do with a half-wild horse."

"He'll be good, Pa, I promise."

"You shouldn't make promises for a horse," Sam grumbled.

"But he *will* be good. I'll take care of him. You'll see."

Pa shrugged. "This horse ain't just for you, Jesse. It's a fair walk up to the Bellawest, and I'd like to ride once in a while. If this horse won't let me do that, he's looking for a new home, y'hear?"

"Yes, Pa."

"Now, fetch him some water and rub him down. I reckon he worked up a sweat as much as we did."

"What's his name?" Jesse asked as Pa and Sam headed for the house.

"Gal who sold him to me said his name's Rio."

Sam barked a laugh. "That suits him just fine."

Jesse nuzzled his face against the horse's side. "Rio. Wild and free, like the river. I like that."

After Jesse spent a couple of hours getting Rio used to him, he wanted to show off his new horse. But school was out for the weekend, so he settled for riding Rio around town. Rio was skittish about being ridden at first. Jesse talked calmly to him and kept stroking his sides until he finally let Jesse mount.

Most folks were busy doing Saturday chores, though they were friendly enough and returned his greetings. Jesse wished more of his schoolmates were out and about. He wanted to show off his fine new stallion. Jesse rode up and down the streets of the town, clucking softly at Rio when the horse got skittish, until he found himself on Eliza's street.

He hoped Allan would be asleep or at least off somewhere doing chores for somebody else. To Jesse's relief, the yard was empty when he arrived. He pulled Rio to a slow walk as he rode by. The house looked still and empty. Maybe the whole family was out for the day.

Jesse led Rio to the next street and turned to the right. He picked up the pace to a trot and rode around the block, slowing again when he got near Eliza's house. There was still no sign of life until he thought he glimpsed Mrs. Matthews at a kitchen window.

Jesse rode around the block again. As he passed the house a third time, he studied the other windows, watching for a twitching curtain, a glimpse of dark hair—anything that might indicate Eliza watched from inside. He imagined her reaction at seeing him seated on Rio. She would be impressed at his skill with a horse. She would dash out of her room, run down the steps, burst out the door, and call after him.

Jesse reached the corner beyond the house. He kicked Rio into a trot and rounded the block to Eliza's street yet again.

As he neared the house, Jesse began to slow, but Rio tossed his head and snorted, stamping and shying away. He whinnied loudly in protest and tensed as if he might break into a run. Jesse was hard-pressed to get Rio back under control as he pulled on the reins to stop the horse.

"What in tarnation do you think you're doing out here?" a voice snapped.

Jesse looked up. He was stopped directly in front of Eliza's house and Boone Evans stood at the end of the walk, in the gate of the picket fence, arms crossed over his chest. The frown on his face seemed out of place when Jesse was so used to a sloppy grin.

Boone looked a little worse for the wear. He was dressed in a rumpled pair of trousers with suspenders hanging off the sides that he must have forgotten to hitch over his shoulders. In place of a shirt, he wore dingy red long johns. His face looked haggard, his eyes dull above dark circles. His ginger hair poked out awkwardly from under his hat. Even the hulking shadow hovering over him seemed to droop and sag.

"I...I..." Jesse stammered.

"You on a carnival merry-go-round or something, kid? You've gone past this house at least six times."

"Four," Jesse corrected.

"Yeah, well, it's about more than my nose can take. You mind riding that smelly thing somewheres else?" Boone waved a hand at Rio, and the horse whinnied and stepped back as if Boone were threatening to hit it.

Jesse jutted out his chin. "I reckon I can ride wherever I want."

Boone leaned against the picket fence wearily. "Look, kid—"

"Jesse!"

"Right. Jesse. I got no more than an hour of sleep last night, and I'm powerful worn out. Your nag there smells like long johns that ain't been washed in a month, with a thick covering of rotting mildew and burnt biscuits. How am I supposed to get any shut-eye with that tickling my nose?"

"I'm sure Mrs. Matthews has a clothespin you can borrow."

Boone raised an eyebrow. "Yeah. Thanks. Where'd you get that smelly beast, anyhow? You didn't have him in town the other day, and I know I ain't smelled him before."

Jesse glanced up at the windows of the house. He thought he saw a curtain move. "My pa bought him off some miner woman today."

Boone stood up straighter, eyes suddenly clear and bright. "Did you say 'miner woman'? That wouldn't be Madge, would it?"

Jesse shrugged. "I dunno. He didn't say her name." He watched the window, trying to decide if he saw Eliza's face behind the curtain or if it was his imagination.

"Stay right there," Boone said. He spun and ran back to the house, leaving the door open behind him.

Jesse stared after Boone. What was that all about? He leaned over slowly and took a good whiff of Rio's mane. He didn't smell anything but the usual horse sweat. What had Boone meant about mildew and biscuits?

Looking back to the window where he thought Eliza might be standing, he realized that it was empty now. Had she turned and left in disgust, agreeing with Boone about Rio's smell? Or was she about to run out the door and apologize, asking to be friends again?

Jesse watched the doorway with anticipation, but the only person to come out a minute later was Boone. He was dressed a little more appropriately now, with a shirt and boots, but his hair still looked wild under the brim of his hat. He carried a gun with a harness, although he didn't strap it on.

As Boone drew near, Rio got jittery again, dancing away from Boone until Jesse got him under control.

Boone took a deep sniff, eyes closed, then gagged. "Whew! It's a wonder I didn't pick up this woman's scent sooner. She smells like a skunk in a rodeo."

Jesse frowned. "A what?"

Boone started down the street, Jesse keeping pace on Rio.

"You want a ride?" Jesse asked.

Boone gave him a sidelong look. "I don't think so. Me and horses, we don't get on too well."

"Where are you going?"

"To find that woman what sold your pa the horse. She was the first one to see this widowmaker everybody talks about. Me and Colorow…" He cleared his throat. "Well, I got a few questions for her."

"Can I come?"

Boone gave him another sideways look. "Only if you leave that nag at home."

Chapter 14
Hot Rocks and Slumgullion Stew

They left Rio at the shed near Jesse's cabin. Pa seemed pleased Jesse had found another friend and offered to rub Rio down so the boys could run off and have their fun.

It was tough for Jesse to keep up with Boone's long strides as they followed the road up into the mountains. They passed Crystal Lake, though not much of it was visible through the thick trees surrounding it. If they kept walking, they would soon reach the entrance to the Bellawest, but Boone abandoned the road and struck off through the trees and underbrush to the left. Every so often, he would stop and take in a deep breath. Then he would grimace and say, "Still on track."

They walked like this for a couple of miles, until the sun was high in the sky and Jesse's stomach rumbled loudly to remind him he'd missed a meal. Through most of the trek, they crashed through the underbrush, following no trail Jesse could see.

"Couldn't you find an easier path?" Jesse grumbled after a branch hit him in the face.

"I follow where the smell leads me," Boone said. "We're getting close."

"How do you know?"

"Believe me." He rubbed his nose. "I know."

They crossed a meadow dotted with red and yellow flowers, veering to the right up a slight incline toward a copse of bright yellow aspen trees. Jesse spotted a thin trail of smoke emerging from the trees.

"Is that what I think it is?" he asked, pointing.

"I reckon so. I think we've found Mad Madge."

"*Mad* Madge?" Jesse looked sharply at Boone. "Is she nuts? You didn't call her 'mad' before."

"Yeah, well, that's what everybody in town calls her."

"Great. We're stumbling into the camp of a crazy lady."

"Just pray she don't have a—" He broke off as a woman stepped out of the trees, peering at them down the barrel of a shotgun.

"—gun," Boone finished quietly, coming to an abrupt stop.

"Hold it right there, you two varmints!" the woman yelled.

She resembled nothing more than a human tumbleweed. Budding wrinkles spread across her face, and her hair was peppered with gray under a squashed wide-brimmed hat. She was dressed in men's overalls with a coat at least two sizes too big. Both were wrinkled and torn, covered in dirt as though she'd been dragged through a mud puddle many times.

"Put down the gun!" she snapped. There were more than a few gaps in her teeth.

Boone slowly bent to set his rifle on the ground. He raised his hands in the air as he stood back up to show he was unarmed.

"What do you got to say for yourselves?" the woman asked.

"We ain't looking for trouble, ma'am," Boone said.

She shifted the shotgun. "Well, you found it. Now, you'd best talk fast. What are you two young'uns doing out here?"

"We're looking for Madge," Boone said.

"My pa bought a horse from her this morning," Jesse added.

The woman's eyes narrowed. "No refunds," she said.

"I wasn't aiming to return him," Jesse said. "He's a right fine horse."

She snorted. "Either you're a glutton for punishment, or you're as crazy as popcorn on a hot skillet."

"Look who's talking," Boone mumbled.

"If you ain't returning the horse, what do you want?" the woman asked.

Boone said, "We just want to talk for a spell, ask about some things she's seen in these hills."

A slow smile spread across the woman's face. It was definitely frightening. "Is that so?" She lowered her shotgun and made a sweeping gesture with one arm. "Boys, this is your lucky day. I'm Madge, and I got stories that'll put hair on your chest! Well, come on now. Don't be shy. You boys like stew?"

Jesse's stomach grumbled again, but Madge didn't give them a chance to answer.

"I got a nice pot of slumgullion on the boil. We'll have a sit-down and a lively chat. Don't leave that rifle out here in the open, son, and mind your head on that tree branch." She waved a hand high in the air above Boone's head. Boone stopped dead in the act of picking up the rifle.

"What?" he asked carefully.

Madge pointed at a tree branch about the same height as the tall shadow around Boone. "You don't want a poke in the eye, now do you? You'll have to duck under a few trees, but my camp is set up in the clearing yonder, so you should be fine once we get there."

Boone looked at Jesse, then back at the woman. "Are you a mage?"

She frowned. "What nonsense you talking?"

"Can you do magic? You know, make things happen that shouldn't?"

"I don't make nothing happen what shouldn't, and you watch your tongue, youngster, or I'll take care of it for you." She waved her gun around for emphasis.

"Yes, ma'am," Boone said hastily, avoiding the barrel of the gun. "But...um, well, can you tell me what you see when you look at me?"

Madge blinked at him. She shook her head at Jesse. "And folks call me crazy. You two are loonier than a fox in a henhouse."

"Please, ma'am."

"Oh, all right, then." She waved a hand up in the air and peered up at Boone's shadowy form. "You look like a regular kid on the outside, but you ain't. I seen a kid like you once, way back when I first come here. She could change into this huge monster, a-flying and spitting fire out of her mouth, though she never hurt me none. She was green, though, and looks like you're..." She narrowed her eyes, as if trying to see past a layer of fog. "Red, I think. You look like an overfed alligator, though I ain't never heard of such creatures this far west, nor this high in the mountains."

Throughout her description, Jesse felt his shock and amazement increase. "You can spit fire?" he asked Boone.

Boone's eyes seemed to bug out of his face. "A girl, you say? Where is she? Is she around here?"

"Naw. She up and took off nigh on to a decade ago. Leastwise, I ain't seen her around these parts since then." She winked knowingly at Boone. "She was right pretty, though."

Boone visibly swallowed. "That don't…" As his voice cracked, he cleared his throat and continued in a lower tone, "That don't matter right now. What's got my insides in a knot is that you can see me—my true form, I mean—even though you don't seem to be a mage, like…"

He looked over at Jesse, and Jesse felt his cheeks grow hot. Did Boone mean that Jesse was a mage? What was a mage?

"I seen a lot more here in these hills," Madge said. "Now, how about a nice bowl of slumgullion and I'll tell you all about it."

"Nice" was not the word Jesse would have used to describe slumgullion. It was a stew made of small animals and weeds that Madge said were edible. After taking a quick sniff in the direction of the pot, Boone swore up and down that dragons only ate rocks, and Madge seemed to believe him.

Her camp was in a clearing amid the quaking aspen, next to a trickle of water that could only be called a stream in the broadest sense of the word. Saddlebags rested against a tree trunk, and a small fire kept the stew hot. A donkey cropped at stray clumps of grass and let out startling brays every so often that made Jesse jump.

Madge nodded toward the donkey. "I bought him in town after I sold Rio to your pa." She chuckled. "Best trade I ever did make."

"You traded a chestnut stallion for that old nag?" Jesse asked.

"You'll get the right of it, boy, after you've tried to ride Rio a couple times."

Jesse jutted out his jaw. "I already rode him, this morning. I didn't have no trouble."

"Yet."

She plopped a bunch of goo onto a tin plate and held it out to Jesse. He gingerly took it along with the spoon she handed over. He was hungry, but he wouldn't be able to choke this stuff down on his deathbed.

"Oh! I clean forgot!" Madge leaped across the stream to her packs and started rummaging around in them. "You boys are in luck!" She pulled out a wad of cloth and opened it up to reveal what looked like lumps of coal. "I whipped up a batch of biscuits this morning." She came back to the fire and plopped one on Jesse's plate. It landed with a dull thud. Jesse stared at it.

"Hence, the smell," Boone mumbled for Jesse's ears alone.

"Well, eat up, eat up," Madge encouraged Jesse.

Jesse plastered on a fake smile and picked up the spoon. As Madge turned back to the fire to dish up another plate of slumgullion for herself, Jesse quickly dumped his behind a nearby rock. Boone choked on a laugh.

Madge turned back around with a biscuit in hand and noticed Jesse's empty plate. "Well, guess that stew hit the spot, eh? Here. Have another scoop."

Before he could stop her, she dumped another heaping spoonful on his plate and tossed on a second biscuit. The donkey hee-hawed like it was a big joke. Boone shook with stifled laughter until Jesse elbowed him in the ribs and he turned his laugh into a cough.

Madge lit into her food as if she hadn't eaten in days. Nobody ever taught her to chew with her mouth closed, and she talked while she ate. She didn't seem to notice when the food dribbled down her chin and hit the collar of her coat.

"Most folks think I'm spinning tall tales when I talk about what I seen here in these hills."

Boone's eyes narrowed. "Just what have you seen?"

Forgetting her food for the moment, she leaned forward eagerly. "There's things the size of a horse. They look like a bear in front and a moose in back. I ain't never heard of them attacking nothing but laundry, though." She gave Jesse an exaggerated wink. "Don't leave your undies hanging out overnight, if you know what I mean."

Jesse choked on a crumb of biscuit.

"That's a shagamaw," Boone said.

Madge tossed the remainder of her mug of coffee onto the fire. It hissed and sizzled. "Then there are these wolf things what looked like they been mashed with a herd of deer. Jumpy and fast as spiders, them critters."

It was hard for Jesse to picture a wolf-deer animal. Even if he saw one, he wasn't sure he would consider it dangerous. More of a joke, really.

"Lucives," Boone supplied. He gave Jesse a sidelong look. "They feed off magic."

"I don't know about magic, but you'd best make sure you got a trusty sidearm if ever you meet one of them." Madge patted her nearby shotgun with emphasis, and Boone fingered the barrel of his rifle.

"What about the widowmaker?" Jesse asked.

Madge blinked at him. "The what?"

Boone said, "I heard tell you was the first to see the widowmaker."

Madge seemed to mull that over for a while, chewing on the inside of her cheek as she frowned in concentration. Jesse could almost see steam coming out of her ears.

"Does it look like a bear, but with a leather hide instead of fur?"

"No," said Boone. "It's a girl, an Indian girl. She's supposed to show up whenever there's a mining accident."

Madge's eyes narrowed. "How do you know about her?"

Boone shrugged. "The story's all over town. Everybody talks about it."

"Whispers about it, more like," Jesse added. "They're all scared of her."

"As well they should be," Madge said.

She stood up and grabbed the plate from Jesse's hands, dumping its contents onto the fire and kicking dirt over it, putting out the flames.

"I should have known Charlie Bassett was a blabbermouth. Come on," she said to them. "There's something you'd best see. Though I warn you, it'll peel the skin off your eyeballs."

Chapter 15
Hard Money

Boone had misgivings about following Mad Madge anywhere, but his curiosity was piqued. He wanted to find out what she knew about the widowmaker, and he had a faint hope she might know something about Colorow, too.

He and Jesse followed Madge deeper into the trees until they came up over a rise on the edge of a small sinkhole. The depression was probably no more than fifty feet across, with a tree growing almost in the center. Long grass waved gently in the breeze, wafting fresh smells toward Boone's nostrils.

Madge cackled and did a little jig that nearly had her tumbling down the bowl of the sinkhole. She capered to the tree and pointed at the roots.

"Down there," she said in a loud whisper that sent spittle flying in every direction. "There lies all your answers."

As Boone got closer, he could make out a dark opening between two of the tree roots where the ground had shifted and made an entrance into the unknown.

"You want us to crawl into a rabbit hole?" Boone asked.

"Might be a tight squeeze," she said, "especially for you, lizard boy. But it'll be worth it, I promise."

"Lizard boy?" Boone grumbled under his breath.

"You ain't about to trust her, are you?" Jesse hissed low enough that Madge wouldn't hear.

Boone shrugged. "What choice do I got? What if she knows something about Colorow disappearing?"

"What if this is some kind of trap, and she's the one who *made* your friend disappear?"

"I reckon that's possible."

"Boone, I don't think we ought to go in that hole."

Madge perched a hand on one hip and glared at them. "What are you all whispering about? You scared?"

Jesse stiffened, and Boone snorted.

"C'mon, you two chicken livers," Madge said. She dropped onto all fours. "I'll show you how it's done."

Suiting actions to words, she shoved her head and shoulders into the hole. She pushed herself in with her feet, breaking the grass and making gouges in the ground. She had obviously done this before, leaving the ground around the hole matted and scraped. In a rush of grunts and groans, she soon disappeared.

"Well?" Jesse asked.

Boone thought about it for a couple of heartbeats. They could take off right now, leave Madge waiting for them underground. If she was the skinwalker, that would be the best course of action. On the other hand, she seemed to know something about the widowmaker. And maybe she could even tell them what had happened to Colorow.

Boone gripped Colorow's gun more tightly. It was dragon-made. That meant it could stand up against anything magical a skinwalker might throw at them. Colorow had left the gun behind in the Ulay. Maybe that's why the skinwalker had gotten the best of him. A man was only as good as his weapon.

Boone squatted down next to the hole. "I'm going in," he said.

Jesse heaved a big sigh and rolled his eyes. "Not by yourself, you ain't," he said as he followed close on Boone's heels.

Boone smiled a little to himself. He really hoped Jesse wasn't the skinwalker. He kind of liked the kid.

Getting into the hole was not exactly easy, especially holding his hat and Colorow's gun. But once Boone managed to squirm past the entrance, it opened out a little into a small tunnel. He still had to crawl, and dirt rained down on him like seven years of bad luck. He didn't want to think about how many baths it would take to get clean after this adventure.

The tunnel gently sloped downhill. He could see a faint light ahead and smelled burning oil mixed with all the other smells he now associated with Madge. At least he was getting used to her stink, so it didn't feel like his nose hairs were curling up and dying anymore whenever he got a whiff of her.

After about thirty feet, the ceiling cut sharply upward, and Boone found himself tumbling down a pile of rock into a larger tunnel big enough for Madge to stand in and hold up a lantern.

Boone got up and brushed off his overalls, grumbling to himself about baths he would never get if he kept this up. A moment later, Jesse plunged down the pile of rock too.

Boone put his hat back on and got showered with dirt. He groaned until Madge pounded him on the back hard enough to make him cough.

"Just good clean dirt, lizard boy. Follow me."

She scampered down the tunnel to the left, humming an off-key melody.

Jesse ran a hand through his hair, dislodging several dirt clods, and shook his hat before replacing it on his head.

"You mind telling me what's important enough that we have to follow this crazy lady into a cave?" he whispered.

They both started down the tunnel after Madge, keeping their voices low as they walked.

"She knows something about the widowmaker," Boone said.

"So? I thought that was just some superstitious legend."

"The widowmaker's real. I seen her."

"What? When?"

"When I was trapped in the Ulay last night. She's the one who got me out."

"Really? How?"

Boone hesitated. How much should he reveal to Jesse? Could he trust him? Colorow had said it was unusual for a thundermage to work the kind of magic that had caused the mining accidents, but it was still possible. And what if Jesse was really a skinwalker, planning to strike as soon as Boone's guard was down? Colorow had gotten after Boone several times for letting his mouth run away with him. Boone was determined that now he was on his own, he wouldn't allow himself to slip up again.

"I don't exactly know how she got me out," Boone said finally. "One minute I was trapped, and the next, I was in the tunnel where them fellas found me."

"But you saw her? The widowmaker?"

"Yeah. I saw her. Indian girl, pretty and young. Smelled like sulphur." Boone winced, wishing he could bite his tongue. But Jesse wouldn't know what a Katsina smelled like.

Madge came to a halt and spun around to face them.

A pile of loose rock and boulders filled most of the tunnel behind her. It looked like there was once a branching tunnel here leading to the left, but the debris completely blocked it.

"That was the real entrance," Madge said, jerking her thumb at the pile of rock. "The cave in wasn't so very long ago, neither."

"How can you tell?" Jesse crouched and fingered one of the rocks at the edge of the debris. "Is the dirt unsettled, or something?"

Madge blinked at him. "I can tell because I saw it happen. That's how."

Spinning back around, she led the way through a narrow opening between the debris and the right tunnel wall. Boone and Jesse hurried to catch up.

"What do you mean?" Boone asked.

Madge's expression was grim. "Five months ago, I was up in this area, looking for the lost Ricas mine. One day, I come upon what looked like the entrance to an old bear cave, but had the markings of human mining about it. So, I thinks to myself, 'Madge, you done found it! This is the Ricas!' So, I goes inside. And I found this."

The tunnel opened up into a large, square chamber. It was big enough that Mrs. Matthews' house would have fit inside, and it was clear full of stuff. Piles of refined ore molded into bars and coins winked from under decaying hides of exotic animals. Boone's eyes widened as he recognized the pelts of leopards and jaguars and other exotic animals from around the world mixed with pelts of magical animals like lucives and shagamaws and schmoos.

There were capes made of bright bird feathers that looked like they might fall to dust if you breathed on them wrong, and fancy headdresses with long tails of feathers and fur.

Stacks of books with metal pages nearly reached the ceiling. In places, the hilts of weapons poked out of the rubble, and Boone thought he could see dragon glyphs on several of them similar to the markings on Colorow's gun. Heaps of armor coated thick with rust lay propped against chests spilling rough pearls and gems. Long, curved blades with jeweled handles and short daggers with jagged edges were piled in one corner. In another, black arrows and spearheads made of flint glinted in the lantern light. There was a smell of dust and decay that made Boone want to sneeze.

"Wow!" Jesse said. He reached out toward a short sword with a glistening silver edge.

Madge grabbed his arm with fingers like claws. "Whoa there, boy. You don't want to be touching this here treasure. It's cursed."

Boone frowned. "What's that supposed to mean?"

She peered up at him, waggling a finger in his face. "You touch any part of this here treasure, and your eyeballs might fall right out of your head. Your toes will curl up, your hair fall out, your tongue—" She stuck out her tongue and grabbed it with a dirty thumb and index finger. Boone winced, imagining the taste. "—'ill 'urn 'ack."

Jesse stared at her. "How do you know?"

"How do I know?" Madge snapped. "'Cause I'm smart, that's why!" Her eyes narrowed shrewdly, and she tapped a temple. "I read petercliffs."

There was a pause as Boone tried to work out what she was talking about.

She rolled her eyes. "You know," she said with exaggerated slowness. "Them pictures on rocks that ancient people carved. Most of them are just for decoration, but this one means something, I can tell."

Boone got a cold feeling in the pit of his stomach. "Maybe you'd best show us," he said.

Madge frowned at him. "C'mon, then. But don't touch nothing unless you want your fingers to fall off."

She walked further into the treasure room. At first, Boone couldn't see how they would get through the piles of treasure without touching anything. But as they moved forward, a path appeared through the loot, and they were able to make it to the other side of the chamber.

As they drew near the far side of the room, Madge's lantern lit up an alcove that hadn't been visible before. Inside, Boone could make out figures chiseled into the rock wall. He swallowed hard. Petroglyphs were often made with dragon magic, driven deep into the rock itself by the chiseling process to bind the magic in place and keep its power potent.

Boone quickly spotted the oval circle with the smaller circles and dots inside that looked so much like a pig snout. Colorow had said that represented the Wité Pot, but there the resemblance between the panels ended. There was another, larger circle above the pot glyph and between two cracks in the rock that was filled with small dots. Another circle, this one filled in, was chiseled above that. To the right and across from the pot glyph, a stick figure, this time with a head and what looked like hair curving off the sides, held up something like a branch with leaves poking out.

Madge pointed to it. "That's the guardian," she said in hushed tones that seemed odd, coming from her. "What folks call the widowmaker now, I guess. She guards the treasure, makes sure nobody touches it or takes it out of here."

"How do you know that's the widowmaker?" Jesse asked.

Madge turned large eyes to him. "I seen her that day I found this cave. She was here, just where you're standing, when I came in the entrance over there."

Boone saw Jesse shudder.

"She seemed surprised to see me. She said something in a language I don't understand."

"Ute?" Jesse asked.

"Naw. Nothing no native folks on earth speak, I don't guess. Then she spoke in English so's I could understand. She said, 'How was it you got past the illusions on the entrance?' 'Course, I didn't know how to answer that. I just said I'd found the place, and was this the Ricas mine? She didn't answer me that, but she said, 'This here treasure is cursed. Them what sees it can't never see the light of day again.' Then she disappeared, and there was rumbling, and all of a sudden I knew it was a cave in. I run back toward the entrance, but I was too late. That big pile of rock blocked my way out. Took me three days to find that back door we come in, and I nearly died of thirst afore I did. So, if'n I was you two young'uns, I'd leave this widowmaker business alone. She's guarding the treasure, and if you mess with her, you won't live to hear no more tales."

It was nearly full dark by the time Boone and Jesse got back to town. Boone declined Jesse's invitation to stay for supper. He was completely worn out. Even the thought of food couldn't rouse him from the stupor that had fallen over his brain.

When he got back to his room at Mrs. Matthews' house, he fell into the bed fully clothed without more than a passing thought for the amount of dirt he shed onto the sheets. He slept until noon the next day.

As he woke to sunshine and the smell of frying bacon, he thought about the petroglyphs Madge had shown them. He could see them clearly in his mind's eye as he lay there slowly drifting out of his dreams. The circles, some filled in, some not; the oval; the big circle on the left with dots inside, and the lines above and below it.

He sat up straight in bed, instantly alert. Scrambling from the tangles of the sheets, he made his way around the room, frantically searching for his hat. When he found it on the floor behind the bed, he heaved a sigh of relief and fetched it out. Fishing in the headband, he pulled out a wrinkled piece of paper.

He had stuffed it inside the band yesterday just before going off with Jesse to hunt down Madge. He figured it might be helpful to record any petroglyphs or other clues he might find so Colorow could examine them when he got back.

Boone walked to the desk and spread the paper out on it, covering up the rubbing he had done in the Ulay. This new rubbing was made with a piece of coal Jesse had found just outside Madge's treasure trove. Boone studied the glyphs. There was the figure Madge was convinced meant the widowmaker on the lower right. Across from it was the sign for the Wité Pot and the circles and lines above it.

What did they mean? Colorow had provided some translation for the glyphs in the Ulay, but Boone couldn't decipher these new figures. Frustrated, he pulled out the paper of glyphs from the Ulay.

He put the two pages side by side and tried to see a pattern in the glyphs, but the smell of bacon kept distracting him. His stomach rumbled. Finally, Boone decided he would do a lot better after one of Mrs. Matthews' excellent meals and a nice hot bath. Then maybe his brain would work right, and he could make sense of the glyphs.

Just when he'd managed to pull on his boots, there was a knock at the door. Mrs. Matthews stood outside, with the sheriff leaning casually against the rail of the landing behind her.

"Mr. Evans, I'm so sorry to disturb you," Mrs. Matthews began.

"It's okay, Mrs. Matthews. I was just headed downstairs anyhow." Boone looked curiously at the sheriff.

Mrs. Matthews cleared her throat. "Sheriff Picket is here about your friend who was lost in the Ulay."

The sheriff stepped forward and extended a hand. "Mr. Evans, I'm truly sorry about the loss of your friend. We've searched the mine from top to bottom and found neither hide nor hair of him. I wanted to let you know, we'll be calling off the rescue efforts for now. We just can't risk more men down there."

Boone clenched his fists at his sides. "I understand, Sheriff."

The sheriff tipped his hat and was about to go when he stopped and turned back to Boone. "By the way, I'll be out of town for a couple of days on business. If anything comes to light concerning your friend, my deputy will let you know."

Boone nodded. He didn't trust his voice to speak as he watched the sheriff go down the stairs. Maybe Colorow really was lost—overcome by the skinwalker, whoever it was. But Boone was determined not to let Colorow's investigation die. Vihala and the other Katsina were counting on him. He would do whatever it took to keep going, even if he had to continue alone.

Chapter 16
See How the Cat Jumps

Jesse woke up on Sunday morning to a rare sunny day. The light streamed in the window and struck him in the face, waking him fairly early, but he was glad to welcome it back as an old friend.

He was more than a little surprised when he rose to find Pa's bed empty. The smell of hot porridge and biscuits came from the front room of the cabin, and Jesse was reminded of Madge's so-called biscuits with her slumgullion stew. He made a face at the memory.

"Does my cooking smell that awful?" Pa asked from the doorway.

"Not your cooking, Pa," Jesse said. "I was just...just thinking."

"Well, you'd best get your head out of the clouds and get a move on or we'll be late for church."

Just before Pa returned to the front room, Jesse realized that Pa was dressed in a clean shirt, his hair washed and slicked back, the whiskers that had sprouted on his chin

165

over the last few days shaved off so only his mustache was left, and this was carefully waxed until the trailing ends came to neat points. Wait. Had Pa said "we'll" be late for church?

Wondering what was going on, Jesse scrambled out of bed and rubbed himself down at the washbasin. Had somebody died? That was the only time Pa could be found in church, if he was paying respects to someone he had known. Jesse shivered with the cold water of the washbasin as he dried his face and arms with a towel. He hoped it wasn't Colorow who had died. Boone would have a rough time with that. Jesse sensed how much Boone missed his friend.

Pa's biscuits weren't as fluffy as Mary's, nor as neatly rounded. They were more like small mountains that were a bit tough on the outside and too doughy in the middle, but they were heaven next to Madge's biscuits, so Jesse ate several with molasses and honey.

When they had washed up after breakfast, Pa walked to the small church house with Jesse. The Reverend Hall was pleased to see Pa and shook his hand warmly.

There was no casket when they entered the little chapel, so Jesse ruled out his theory that Pa was coming to church to attend a funeral.

Mary seemed pleasantly surprised to find them already seated in the chapel when she and Sam arrived, and Sam was positively shocked. His jaw dropped open when he saw Pa and Jesse sitting on a pew halfway between the door and the pulpit. Pa jumped up to let Sam and Mary sit by the window. The four of them fit on the bench with just a little room to spare.

Mrs. Matthews came in with Eliza and Allan in tow. They sat in their usual spot, the front bench to the right. Neither child looked at Jesse as they swept past. Eliza sat down and seemed to huddle on the bench, as if she felt sick.

"Is this seat taken?" Jesse looked up to see Miss Dalton standing in the aisle. She was dressed in a frilly blue outfit with a bustle on the back. Her hair was piled high, stray ringlets framing her face, with a fancy hat topping it all.

Pa and Sam stumbled to their feet, and after a moment, Jesse followed suit.

"Good day, Miss Dalton," Mary said.

"Miss Dalton," Sam echoed.

"Do you mind if I sit by you?" Miss Dalton asked. "Most of the other benches are full."

Jesse glanced around the church. He could see several benches far less crowded than theirs.

"Not at all," Pa said.

They all moved over until Jesse felt like a sardine in a can. Miss Dalton sat down next to him, her gloved hands folded primly in her lap, enveloping Jesse in the scent of roses.

From Jesse's other side, Pa cleared his throat. "You're looking lovely today, Miss Dalton."

"Why, thank you, Mr. Owens."

"I hope my boy is behaving himself in your class."

Miss Dalton smiled at Jesse, and he felt his cheeks grow hot. "He's a good student."

"Thanks to your efforts, I'm sure."

"Mr. Owens, you're too kind." She laughed, a low musical burst, as she dropped her eyes modestly to her lap. Her cheeks became tinged with pink and she picked at a ribbon on her handbag, fraying it into shreds.

"The weather's fine today, ain't it?" Pa continued.

"The best we've had for many days. It will be perfect for the picnic."

"Are you..." Pa cleared his throat and started again. "Have you been invited to sup with anybody yet?"

She batted her eyes at Pa. Jesse realized she had very long lashes and dark eyes, like liquid pools of coal. "Why no, Mr. Owens, I haven't."

"Then I hope you'll join us for the picnic."

Jesse felt his heart drop into his toes. Pa had just invited Jesse's *teacher* to have a picnic with them? Suddenly, Jesse realized why Pa had gotten up so early and made the effort to come to church. He was sweet on Miss Dalton!

"We'd love to have you with us," Mary said, smiling warmly at Miss Dalton. "It will be nice to have the company of another woman."

Mary elbowed Sam, and he added hastily, "We'd be pleased if you joined us, Miss Dalton."

Reverend Hall passed them on his way to the pulpit as Miss Dalton inclined her head. "Then I'd be delighted to join you. Thank you for the invitation."

Jesse thought he might be sick right there on the chapel floor.

Jesse was miserable the entire rest of the morning. Church services were more of a torture than ever. He felt like a third wheel sitting between Pa and Miss Dalton. Her rose-scented perfume suffocated him. Eliza never looked back at him, not even once, though Jesse caught Allan's eye a couple of times. Allan's expression was unreadable.

When church was over, Pa asked Jesse to help gather the picnic supplies. No one else could approach Rio without getting nipped, so Jesse strapped the picnic basket to the horse and led him up the road into the mountains with many of the other townsfolk. The sun still shone, warming the soggy ground, but Jesse could no longer enjoy it.

They made their way to the picnic spot by Crystal Lake. Pa walked beside Miss Dalton several feet behind the rest of them. Jesse couldn't hear what they said, but he heard her laugh every so often, and it only made him angrier each time he heard it.

When they reached the lake, they followed the crowd to a grassy area on the east side where families spread blankets and began unpacking baskets.

Mary pointed out an empty spot and Jesse obediently led Rio to it, where Sam helped unload the horse. Mary and Miss Dalton spread out an orange gingham blanket on the ground while Jesse led Rio to a nearby cluster of bog birch and tied him up where he could crop at the grass.

Rio whinnied in protest as Jesse started to leave him there. Turning back, Jesse patted the horse's flank and stroked its nose. He would ten times rather spend the day with Rio than watch Pa flirting with Miss Dalton.

"Jesse!" Mary called when Jesse continued to hesitate. "I got fried chicken and apple pie!"

Jesse's stomach rumbled, and he decided to join the group just long enough to woof down some food. Then he would take Rio for a ride.

There were at least fifteen other families spread across the grassy area near the lake. Some of the children had taken off their shoes and stockings to frolic at the water's edge, splashing each other playfully.

The women sat pertly on their blankets wearing large hats to shade their faces and dished out picnic food to everyone. Some of the men scampered with the children, playing tag or leapfrog. Talk and laughter flew back and forth across the picnic ground. The cheerful atmosphere grated on Jesse's nerves. He felt out of place and awkward. He wanted to be alone.

"...and he said he'd rather bet the farm and the whole horse and caboodle," Pa was saying as Jesse approached the blanket.

Miss Dalton laughed and laid a hand on Pa's arm. "Oh, Paul, that's the funniest thing I ever heard!"

Jesse suddenly lost his appetite. Miss Dalton was now on a first-name basis with Pa?

Mary held out a chicken leg to Jesse. "Come sit down, Jesse," she said.

Jesse shuffled his feet as eight pairs of adult eyes turned to him.

"I ain't...I ain't hungry. Can I take Rio for a ride, Pa?"

Pa frowned. "I reckon so, son. Are you sure you don't want some of Mary's picnic lunch first? You ain't never turned down her cooking before."

"I just..." He looked down at Miss Dalton and saw the concern in her expression. "I'll be back after a while, I promise."

Jesse ignored the puzzled frowns they gave each other and turned away.

Rio seemed pleased to see Jesse back so soon. Jesse untangled Rio's lead from the bog birch and was about to mount when he heard angry voices coming from further into the trees. Pulling Rio along behind him, Jesse walked toward the voices to investigate.

After about thirty yards, he saw a clearing open ahead through the trees. Jesse stopped and threw Rio's lead over a branch before ducking behind a berry bush to watch.

The clearing ahead wasn't large, not as big as the area where the town picnicked on the east side of the lake. There was a large boulder that overhung what looked like a crawl space on the far end of the clearing, and the shore of the lake sloped gently down to the water there. Jesse could see across the smooth surface of the lake to the island that rose in the center, covered with trees. Most of the trees in this area were ponderosa or spruce evergreens, growing straight and tall and thick.

In the center of the clearing, a few steps from the lake's edge, Zeke and two of his buddies surrounded Allan. Allan's whole body radiated barely controlled rage as Zeke and his friends taunted him.

"You ain't so smart now, are you," Zeke sneered, "without that teacher lady and your friends around."

"Where is my sister?" Allan growled. "What did you do to her?"

"My pal took her for a friendly ride into the canyon. There's an old abandoned mine up there."

It felt like Jesse had swallowed a lead weight. Zeke had kidnapped Eliza?

"She'll be nice and cozy underground in the dark," Zeke continued, "where nobody can see that freak face of hers."

Allan put his head down like an angry bull. Roaring, he charged at Zeke, knocking him over backward onto the ground. Fists started flying. It would have been an even match, but Zeke's friends joined in the fray. Soon, Allan was getting a sound beating.

Jesse hesitated another moment. He had tried to help Eliza with these bullies once before, and Allan had been anything but grateful. In fact, Allan had been downright hostile from the moment Jesse had met him. But as he watched Zeke's friends kick Allan and punch him in the face, Jesse knew he couldn't stand by any longer.

Rushing forward, he tackled the nearest boy and threw him to the ground, giving him a taste of his own medicine before he felt arms twisting through his to pull him back. Zeke's two buddies held Jesse in place while Zeke paced around to face him.

"This ain't your fight, new kid," Zeke said, "so I suggest you turn right on around and head back to the picnic before you regret it."

Allan groaned and looked up at Jesse. "What are you doing?"

Jesse firmed his jaw. "Evening out the odds," he said.

Wiping at the stream of blood running from his nose, Allan shifted and tried to stand, wincing. "I had it under control," he said.

"Is that so?" Jesse asked.

Zeke spun around and threw a punch at Allan's middle that made him double over, groaning in pain. "Nobody said you could get up!" Zeke yelled.

Hooking a foot behind the leg of one of his captors, Jesse pulled the boy off balance. The boy let go with a cry, and Jesse swung his free arm around to land a sound blow against the shoulder of the other boy, who also let go.

Then Jesse was in the thick of it. He threw punches right and left, landing blows more often than not, but all three boys surrounded him now, trying to pin his arms and throwing punches of their own. Jesse thought he might soon be overwhelmed, just as Allan was earlier. An especially vicious kick brought him to his knees in the mud and he thought he heard the roar of thunder, although it might have been no more than a ringing in his head.

Then Allan was there, pulling the other boys off Jesse with a guttural yell. He landed blow after blow and beat back Zeke's two friends to the edge of the trees. Jesse scrambled to his feet to face Zeke.

"You're gonna die!" Zeke growled.

Jesse didn't waste time arguing. He threw a blow to Zeke's ribs, but Zeke didn't slow as he made a grab for Jesse's torso. They went down and rolled a couple of times on the ground. Gasping for breath under Zeke's weight, Jesse blocked a punch aimed at his nose. Zeke's fist glanced off Jesse's ear.

They rolled into the water's edge, but Jesse barely registered getting wet as Zeke landed a blow to his side and knocked the wind out of him. Jesse gasped for breath. Zeke ploughed a left hook into Jesse's face, knocking his head to the side. He felt blood spurt from his nose, and suddenly Jesse's fists were flying. Thunder cracked loudly overhead and the wind whipped around them, threatening to carry them off, but Jesse hardly noticed.

He was like a wild man. The anger and frustration he had held in check for so long came rushing to the surface, and he was full of strength. He plowed his fists into Zeke's torso, his head, his arms. Soon, Zeke was the one on the ground, trying to avoid Jesse's fists. But Jesse didn't stop. He couldn't stop. The onslaught of his anger was too great. It was like a raging river that had been set free of its banks, crushing and destroying everything in its path.

Zeke huddled in the mud, squealing in a high-pitched voice like a little girl, until Jesse felt someone grab his arms from behind, yanking him back.

As soon as Jesse's fists stopped landing blows, Zeke crawled away.

"C'mon!" one of Zeke's friends yelled over the wind. "We gotta get out of here!"

He helped Zeke stand and they half-ran, half-limped out of the clearing. A thunderclap, loud enough to shake the ground, cracked open the skies above.

Jesse yanked against the arms that held him fast and screamed after Zeke as loud as he could.

"Stop!" Pa's voice said. He sounded angrier than Jesse had ever heard him. "Jesse Benjamin Owens, that is e-*nough*!"

Pa's grip on his arms threatened to break the bones if Jesse continued to fight. He clenched his teeth, forcing himself to stop moving, to hang limp in Pa's grip. He tasted blood in his mouth and realized it flowed freely from his nose. Slowly, Jesse's surroundings came into focus.

It didn't look like the same place where the fight had started. Dark clouds swirled and writhed overhead. Jagged forks of lightning split the sky in rapid succession, hitting the trees around the lake and setting fire to the needles. Tree limbs fell to the ground with loud cracks. A fierce wind bent the treetops almost double and whipped the lake into a frenzy.

Rio yanked against his lead, still stuck around the tree branch. He whinnied and pawed at the ground, the whites of his eyes showing his fear.

Allan stood panting at the edge of the clearing, staring up at the sky in horror. "I gotta go find Eliza!" he yelled as he ran away.

"What happened?" Jesse panted.

"A horrible storm come up. We gotta take shelter."

"Is…" Jesse swallowed hard. "Is anybody hurt?"

"Nobody but that boy you was beating into the ground."

Pa's grip on Jesse's arms loosened enough that Jesse was able to pull free. He stumbled a few feet away, wiping the blood from his face with his arm.

"It's starting again, ain't it?" Pa asked. "The storms, the ice, the wind. I thought things were different here. That life would be better."

Jesse started trembling and rubbed his arms where Pa's grip had bruised the flesh. "Life ain't better here," he said. "I wish we'd never left Kansas. I wish we'd never come here. I want to go home, Pa."

"There ain't nothing left in Kansas for us but painful memories, son."

Jesse turned and glared at Pa. "How can you say that? How can you forget Ma so soon?" His words were punctuated by a crack of thunder.

"What fool nonsense are you talking?"

"I saw you with Miss Dalton!" Jesse spat. "How can you make calf eyes at her with Ma not even cold in her grave?"

"You watch your tongue, boy!" Pa took a step forward, hand going up as if he meant to strike Jesse.

The area around them suddenly froze, the ice growing as if winter had arrived in fast motion. Ice crusted the plants around them, the bushes, the trees. It pulled down the branches and leaves with its weight. Rio seemed more frightened than ever, stomping his feet and whinnying frantically, fighting the tether.

Pa stopped dead in his tracks, staring at the frost that glistened on the ground between him and Jesse. "How are you doing this?" he whispered.

Jesse's trembling grew worse. He felt his teeth chattering with the cold as his breath fogged in front of his face. "I don't know," he said with a choked sob.

Pa looked up at the sky, the roiling clouds and lightning, at the frozen trees cracking and groaning in the wind that still pushed at them, threatening to break them clean in half. "Nobody controls the weather," he said.

Jesse felt the next flash of lighting coming, a sensation of loss as electricity ran out of him and shot into the sky, then came back down in a fork of lightning. "I control the weather," he said, realizing it for the first time with a sense of horror. Suddenly, everything made sense—the constant rain when he felt miserable, the sunshine when he was happy, the storm when he was angry or upset. He didn't know how he did it, or how to stop it, but he knew in that moment that it was true.

Pa barked a laugh that had no humor in it. "That's impossible, Jesse." His words had a bitter edge, as if he were trying to convince himself that water ran uphill.

"I don't know how, Pa, but I can."

"Don't be daft, boy!" Pa jabbed a finger at Jesse. "There ain't no mortal man with that kind of power!"

His shout startled the already frightened Rio. With a mighty yank, the horse broke the rope and lunged into a gallop, racing past them and into the trees to the north.

"Rio!" Without thinking, Jesse ran after him.

"Jesse!" Pa yelled.

Suddenly, a staccato pattering came from the east. Jesse looked back over his shoulder to see a bank of black clouds mushrooming toward them. Below the dark clouds, huge balls of ice fell from the sky, hitting the trees below and breaking off limbs with loud cracks like gunshots.

Jesse pointed. "Pa!" he yelled.

Pa looked back and saw the clouds. He motioned toward the overhanging boulder. There was just enough room under it for two people. "Get back here!" he shouted.

Jesse hesitated. Rio couldn't fit under that boulder. But maybe they could outrun the storm together, if Jesse could catch him. Jesse broke into a hard run.

"Jesse!" Pa screamed. "Jesse!"

Jesse bent his head forward, running for all he was worth. He felt the wind rushing past his ears, pulling tears from his eyes. He had to catch Rio.

He could see the horse ahead. Lightning hit a tree, and it crashed to the ground a few feet in front of Rio. The horse veered to the right. Jesse changed course to intercept, pushing his legs to go faster. Faster. If only the horse would stop running long enough that Jesse could catch him!

A fork of lightning broke the sky, hitting the ground directly in front of Rio with a booming crack of thunder. The horse skidded to a stop and sunfished, his forelegs pawing the air. Jesse caught up to him and grabbed for the reins. Yanking hard, he brought the horse back down to earth.

Aware of the pounding hailstones sweeping nearer, Jesse scrambled into the saddle. He kicked the horse's flanks.

"Heeyah!"

Rio took off again like a bullet from a gun, but this time Jesse had him under control. The trees around them became a blur. The lightning flashed overhead, and the sky roiled with clouds. It felt like Jesse was riding through a nightmare.

Jesse could hear the hail gaining on them even over the noise of the storm. If they didn't find shelter soon, they would get hit by monstrous balls of ice big enough to kill a man.

Jesse bent low over Rio's neck.

"C'mon, boy!" he yelled.

Not that Rio needed more urging to run faster. The horse gave it everything he had, neck stretched out, hooves flying. But it wasn't enough. Glancing back over his shoulder, Jesse saw the black clouds overtaking them. In another second, they would get hit with the hail.

Then he sensed something swoop past them. Jesse looked up and saw a huge red figure falling out of the sky toward them. Its general shape resembled the shadow that always hovered over Boone, only this was no shadow. The creature was covered in red scales. It was at least as big as a railroad car or a small house. It had leathery wings spread wide, catching the wind and shifting to stay on course in the gale. The monster opened its long, alligator-like snout to reveal a row of sharp, pointed teeth and roared loud enough that the ground trembled. Its legs were tucked underneath its body, one foot clutching a rifle, while its arms stretched forward, claws spread wide. With a growing sense of horror, Jesse realized the thing meant to grab him.

Chapter 17
Going for a Joy Ride

B oone thought that saving someone's life would have easily qualified him for a little gratitude and praise. He swept down out of the sky like an avenging angel and grabbed Jesse, the horse, and all. He flew them to the entrance of the Bellawest, where they would be safe from the hailstorm that hit a moment later, filling the mine entrance with a deafening clatter.

And what did Boone get for this heroic act? A tongue lashing from Jesse and a kick in the shin from the ornery mule of a horse just before it spun away from Boone to go galloping off into the dark.

"What in tarnation do you think you're doing?" Jesse's yell echoed off the rock walls.

Boone quickly shifted to his human form, setting down Colorow's gun and spreading his hands out in a calming gesture. "Jesse, it's me, Boone."

Jesse hardly seemed to notice. "You scared Rio half to death!" He spun on a boot heel and ran after the horse.

Boone harrumphed and followed Jesse. He didn't have to go far.

Forty yards in, the tunnel narrowed enough that the horse couldn't go any further. Wooden beams bracing the ceiling marched away into darkness, like the ribs of a dead animal.

Jesse held the horse's reins, stroking its nose and talking softly to it. As soon as Boone approached, however, the horse threw itself back on its hind legs, snorting and whinnying.

"Back off!" Jesse yelled. "Just back off, Boone."

"Okay, okay." Boone retreated until he couldn't see them anymore, but he could tell the horse had calmed down when it stopped raising such a ruckus. Stupid smelly animal.

Boone sat down by the entrance, staring out at the storm. The hail stopped a few minutes after it hit, turning to a fierce rain that gradually became a gentle patter. Boone could see the broken branches of trees littering the slope below the mine under piles of ice left from the hail. The rain soon dissolved the ice, leaving a muddy slope in its wake.

After a while, Rio's smell got stronger, and Boone heard the echoing clops of the horse's hooves on the rock. Jesse appeared, leading Rio, and looped the horse's rope around a rock outcropping several feet behind Boone. The horse snorted in protest, rolling its eyes at Boone, but it didn't panic again.

Jesse came forward and sat down next to Boone. "I'm sorry I yelled," he said quietly. "It's just that you scared Rio."

Boone watched the storm outside. "Scared you too, I reckon."

Jesse ran a hand through his hair. He'd lost his hat somewhere along the way. They were silent for several moments. The storm was passing, clouds more of the normal gray variety, the rain falling ever more gently.

Finally, Jesse jutted his chin at the sky. "I did that," he said. "I made that storm."

"I know," Boone said.

Jesse turned sharply to look at Boone.

"You're a mage, ain't you?" Boone said.

"A what?"

"A mage is somebody with uncommon power. Some folks call it magic."

Jesse snorted. "Magic?"

"Yeah, magic. There are different types of magic that work different ways, controlling the elements and such. Now you, you're a rare piece of work. You control more than one thing at a time, like bringing together different parts of a storm when you manage the weather. Ain't nobody seen that kind of power for a couple hundred years. We call you a thundermage."

Shaking his head, Jesse mumbled. "I must be going crazy."

"Well, mages only go crazy on Tuesdays and this here is Sunday, so I reckon you're safe...for a couple of days, anyhow."

Jesse stared at him, and Boone couldn't keep the grin off his face. Finally, Jesse started to smile.

"You're a regular hoot, ain't you?" Jesse asked. "So tell me this, lizard boy." Boone winced at the nickname Mad Madge had given him. "If I got so much magic, how come I ain't always been able to control the weather?"

"You couldn't use your magic until that lightning hit you."

Jesse's grin fled like a rabbit before a coyote. "I didn't even tell Pa about that. How'd you know?"

"Because that's how a mage gets his power. Something awful happens that wakes up the magic in you, and you call up the storm that jump-starts your power." Boone swallowed hard, keeping his eyes on the rain. "You wanna talk about it?" he finally asked.

A heavy silence hung over them as they both watched the rain create tiny rivers that ran down the slope in the mud away from the entrance.

When Jesse started to speak, it was so soft that Boone almost couldn't make out the words. "It was last spring, about four months ago. Ma was expecting a baby in a couple of months. Pa needed to go into town for supplies. I had some pocket change for a licorice whip, and I begged to go with him. He said no. He didn't want Ma left alone. I was mad. After Pa left, I ran off to go fishing in the stream a couple of miles from our farm. When I got back, Pa and the doc were there. See, Ma was thrown from her horse when she started out to come looking for me. She was hurt real bad, and the baby came too soon. It was a girl, but it never drew breath. Ma wrapped it in yellow gingham and held it in her arms, singing a lullaby. She was still singing when she died."

The rain fell gently outside. Boone pretended not to see the tears running down Jesse's cheeks.

"That's when I ran," Jesse continued. "I didn't even notice the storm brewing, not until the lightning hit me. When I came to, I thought maybe I was dead. I wanted to be dead, to be with Ma and the baby. As I lay there, thinking about it, the storm around me got worse and worse. Pretty soon, there was tornadoes touching down everywhere. It was like I was dreaming. They spun off in all directions. I didn't know how to stop them."

"Once you start a storm, you can't stop it, from what I understand," Boone said. "But in time, you can learn to control it."

Jesse shook his head. "Pa never blamed me for Ma's death, but I've always known it was my fault, just like that storm was my fault. It killed people, Boone." He buried his face in his hands. "I killed people."

Boone hesitated, then patted Jesse awkwardly on the shoulder. "It weren't your fault. Don't think that now. When a mage first gets his power, he ain't to blame for what happens. Most of the time, he don't even know he's doing it. The Katsina, they'll train you up proper, help you get control of the magic so's you can use it for good."

"Katsina?" Jesse asked.

"They're mages too, only they been around for a few more years than you and me. Since I'm a dragon, that's saying something. The Katsina watch over the magic in these here western parts. They make sure nobody uses it wrong. Now, as for your ma's death, well, it was tragic, no doubt about it, but it weren't just because you took off to go fishing for a couple hours. When my mama disappeared, I thought for years I'd done something to make her angry so she didn't love me no more. It took me a long time to come to the realization that she didn't leave because of me.

It was because of her, who she was, the decisions she made."

Jesse sniffed. "How old were you?"

"I wasn't much past a babe in my mama's arms."

After a moment, Jesse asked softly, "Boone, does the pain ever go away?"

Boone wrapped his arms around himself to ward off the chill. "Not really. But after a while, you don't think about it every second of the day no more. Just every so often, it'll jump out and stab you, like a knife in the gut."

They were silent after that, watching the sky as the clouds spent themselves and finally started to drift apart.

"I gotta go find Pa." Jesse tightened Rio's saddle and stroked the horse's flank. He could feel deep down in his bones that the storm had passed, and he was anxious to get out of the Bellawest.

Boone stood up and brushed off his trousers. "I saw your pa duck under a big rock just afore I carried you off," he said. "I reckon he was safe from the storm there."

"Just the same, I don't want him to worry none about me," Jesse said.

"Suit yourself."

Boone climbed to his feet, his long limbs unraveling like a length of knotted string, and tipped his hat onto his head. As he did, two folded papers fluttered to the ground. Jesse bent to scoop them up. Markings on the papers caught his eye as he held them out to Boone.

"What's that?" Jesse asked. Then he reddened as he realized it wasn't his business. "You don't have to tell me if you don't want."

Boone opened the papers and smoothed them out. "Naw, I don't mind. Fact is, maybe you can help me figure it out. I never been much good at writing."

"Neither am I, but I could give it a go."

He took the papers Boone handed him and peered at them. One paper he recognized as the rubbing Boone had done in Madge's treasure cave. The crude drawings stood out on the paper, a stark contrast to the black background.

The other paper was similar, except this one had a red background instead of black. Jesse saw circles within circles and a figure similar to the one on the other paper, except this one had no head.

"Are these all peter…" He laughed at his unconscious imitation of Madge. "I mean, petroglyphs?"

"Yep." Boone pointed at an oval shape on the left with two circles and a bunch of dots inside. "Colorow said this symbol is a pot he came here to find. And this line up here, with the curved lines coming out the bottom, well, I reckon that could be rain or something. Maybe, since that person is holding what looks like a plant, it means rain watering crops?"

Jesse cocked his head as he studied the paper. "Yeah," he said slowly. "I guess I can see how that looks like a plant being watered, but what if it's a hand, reaching down?"

Boone seemed to get excited. "Hey, maybe you're right!"

"Where'd you see these other drawings?" Jesse asked, pointing to the red paper.

"Them symbols were in a cave in the Ulay mine, up the road a piece. Me and Colorow found them just afore..." He swallowed, and his voice got quieter. "Just afore the accident."

Jesse realized Boone was still upset over his friend's disappearance. Not wanting to embarrass Boone, Jesse focused hard on the papers, turning one upside down, then the other, then straightening them back out. The pictures could mean any number of things. Finally, he pointed to an upside-down triangle on the first sheet.

"This one kind of looks the same as that person Madge thought was the widowmaker," he said, "except it don't have a head, like this other fellow."

"Really?" Boone peered at the three symbols. He tipped his hat back. "I do believe you're right. I don't know what that means, though."

Jesse's brow furrowed in concentration. "Who do you reckon drew these pictures?"

Boone seemed very sure of himself as he answered, "Dragons. It's our way of writing—the way we sometimes work magic, too."

"Then how come you can't read it?"

Boone squirmed and shuffled a toe in the dirt. "I wasn't raised by dragons. The Katsina are trying to teach me magic, but I ain't exactly a quick study."

Jesse frowned down at the papers. "Maybe magic would help you decipher these."

Boone snorted. "My magic don't work that way, and you're just a greenhorn. You don't know how to work magic proper yet."

Jesse felt a sudden eagerness. If he could learn to control his magic, maybe he could use it for something useful. "You could teach me!"

Boone's face reddened. "I, uh, I'm just trying to learn it myself."

"You're a mage, like me?"

"Not yet. I reckon someday I'll be."

"How do you fly, then?"

"I'm a dragon."

"But don't you use magic?"

"Dragons *are* magic. We don't need no spells to use it."

"Then why do you have to learn about it?"

Boone paused, his mouth hanging open as if trying to think of a reply. Finally, he said, "Dragons who learn to use spells, like you humans, can make stuff, powerful stuff that works magic all its own. But I can't do that without training. These glyphs," he pointed at the drawings, "I need to learn them afore I can make anything useful with my magic."

"I wish I could help more." Jesse handed the papers back to Boone. "But I don't even read English so good. Eliza was helping me before—" He broke off, remembering the fight in the clearing with Zeke and Allan.

"Eliza!" he shouted. "I forgot! Zeke said his friend took Eliza to some abandoned mine somewhere in a canyon. We gotta find her!"

Jesse ran to the lip of the entrance, looking down at the muddy slope that led steeply to the clearing below and the buildings of the mine operation.

"Might be dangerous, going down that way," Boone said. "You ain't gonna find that girl if you fall and break your neck."

"How else do we get out of here?"

Boone grinned. "I could carry you."

Jesse stepped back, waving his arms in protest. "I had enough of that once. I ain't doing it again!"

"Why not?" There was a mischievous glint in Boone's eye. "You chicken?"

"I ain't chicken!" Jesse protested hotly. "And you'd best watch your mouth, or else I'll hit you with a whirlwind or something."

Boone tucked his hands into his armpits and flapped his elbows. "Bock, bock, bock, *bock*!"

"Well, what about Rio?" Jesse said, fishing for an excuse to avoid another frightening ride like the one he'd experienced earlier. "Last time, you nearly gave him a heart attack."

"Serves him right, the ornery mule," Boone said.

Now Jesse really was angry. "If Rio ain't going, I ain't going!"

"Okay, okay. Maybe if I knocked him upside the head so he was out cold when I picked him up?"

Jesse glared at Boone with all the venom he could muster.

"I guess that ain't such a good plan."

"What do you got against horses, anyhow?"

"It ain't me. It's them. They don't take kindly to the smell of an overgrown flying snake."

Jesse crossed his arms over his chest and stared out the entrance. He could see the smelter building far below in the clearing beside the road. A hefty iron car hung against the building from a cable that led to the entrance.

"Can you get that mining car up here?" Jesse asked.

Boone looked around and spotted the car below. "You fixing to put the horse in that? Believe me, it would be far easier and less painful if I just picked up the dumb animal and flew him down to the ground."

"But you smell like a flying snake. I can cover Rio's eyes to keep him from getting scared in a mining car, but I can't hide his nose from your smell."

"I was wrong," Boone said. "I think mages really do go crazy on Sundays."

"Are you going to help me or not?"

"Fine. But you'd best take that animal far back in the tunnels afore I transform lest I give him that heart attack."

Jesse suppressed a smile and led Rio back into the tunnel to where it became too narrow for the horse to pass. He patted Rio's side and rubbed his nose.

"I'll be back soon for you, boy," he whispered.

When he got back to the entrance, it was blocked by a huge form. Even though Jesse expected it, seeing Boone as a dragon was still a shock. Two thick, curling horns thrust up through previously hidden holes in Boone's hat. His muzzle was covered in ginger fur that also ran down his neck. A long tail that ended in a sharp-looking barb twitched gently on the ground. Close up, Jesse could see that Boone's red scales were flecked with gold that glistened. Boone's rifle hung from one thick forearm.

The huge alligator head swung toward Jesse, the mouth opening. For a split second of terror, Jesse thought he was about to get eaten, or maybe roasted alive, but then Boone's voice came out of the dragon's mouth.

"You coming?" he asked.

"What? Me? I thought this was your deal."

The dragon jaws gaped in what Jesse hoped was a smile. "You don't want to miss out on all the fun."

Jesse swallowed hard. "I ain't no bird to go twittering off through the sky."

"It's just like riding a horse, only better."

"How would you know?"

"So, you *are* chicken."

"Nobody calls me chicken. Especially not some overgrown lizard boy."

Grinding his teeth to fight off the fear, Jesse strode forward. Boone crouched lower on the ground, leaving enough clearance between his back and the roof of the mine for Jesse. Jesse placed one foot on the dragon's shoulder and grabbed the joint of a wing he could just reach, hoisting himself up and onto the dragon's back. The scales were slippery and firm. Jesse had a passing fear that he would slide right back off, but he hooked his knees under the joints of the wings and grabbed on to a tuft of fur at the base of Boone's neck. Boone didn't seem to mind.

"Hang on tight," Boone said.

"Don't worry." Jesse gasped as Boone shifted and moved beneath him. He was hanging on to Boone's fur so hard that his knuckles were white.

Boone leaped out of the entrance, spreading his wings at the same time. Jesse bit off a scream as the ground came rushing toward him and his stomach dropped into his toes. Then the wind caught Boone's wings, and the fall turned into a glide. They scooped back up into the sky, and then they were soaring over the mountains.

Jesse tried not to look straight down at the ground so far below them. Instead, he kept his eyes on the clouds above and the mountain peaks. They looked almost close enough to touch. He took in a deep breath of clean, cold air. It smelled good and fresh, almost as though the sky were apologizing for its earlier temper tantrum.

Boone swooped close to one of the peaks, swiping at it with one claw and grabbing a wad of snow. He threw it back in Jesse's face, laughing.

Jesse shook his head and spluttered, but didn't dare let go of Boone's fur to brush away the snow. It was cold and wet. He licked at it with his tongue.

Then Boone was plunging back to earth, the treetops rushing at them so fast that tears leaked out of Jesse's eyes. Just before they crashed into the trees, Boone pulled up, swooping over them and back up into the sky. Jesse's stomach was doing flip-flops, but he realized he liked the sensation. He started to laugh.

Boone said something that was snatched away by the wind.

"What?" Jesse hollered.

"Hang on!" Boone yelled, louder this time.

Jesse took a firmer hold of Boone's fur and gripped the wing joints tight with his knees. Then they were rolling through the sky, doing loops that made the world spin. Jesse squeezed his eyes shut and screamed with joy.

When they came out of the spin, they were both laughing hard. Jesse's sides hurt. He couldn't remember the last time he'd actually laughed. It felt good. It felt right.

Boone's laugh cut off suddenly.

"What's the matter?" Jesse shouted.

Boone banked to the left. "We gotta take a detour," he yelled. "I think I just seen the widowmaker!"

Chapter 18
Hightailing it Three Ways from Sunday

This far in the air, Boone couldn't smell the figure he saw far below, so he wasn't sure he'd really seen the widowmaker. But he could tell it was a girl in the canyon below, wearing a brownish dress, with braided black hair. He wasn't about to take chances.

Making for a ridge overlooking the river, Boone glided gently down to earth. This was no time for the shenanigans he'd done to impress Jesse. He landed a few feet back from the ridge in a meadow dotted with purple wildflowers that had an oversweet scent, like rotting leaves.

Jesse slid off Boone's back and made for the ridge, throwing himself down on his belly the last couple of feet to crawl forward and peer over the edge. After a few minutes, Jesse shimmied back from the edge and stood up, brushing dirt and plants off his clothes.

"She's coming this way," he said.

Boone lashed his tail. "I wish I could smell her," he grumped. "Then I'd know if it really is the widowmaker."

Jesse cocked his head to one side. "Have you smelled the widowmaker before?"

"Oh, yeah."

The clink of loose shale and rustling leaves came from the other side of the ridge.

Jesse spun to stare at the ridge. "How'd she get up here so fast?"

Boone realized suddenly that if he transformed back to his human shape this close to the widowmaker, she would sense his magic, just as he could smell hers. He looked frantically around the meadow and spotted a huge pile of boulders on the north edge. Steam came out of the ground near one of the boulders, but he ignored it. In two bounds, he landed behind the rocks and crouched as low as he could. He could still see Jesse through a crack in the boulders.

Jesse spoke as a figure came up over the ridge. "Eliza!" he said in a shocked voice.

As the girl stepped forward and faced Jesse, Boone realized that she was that girl with the scarred face, Mrs. Matthews' daughter. It was easy to see how he had been fooled. Her hair was dark, just like the widowmaker's, and ran down her back in two long braids.

"Are you okay?" Jesse blurted. "Zeke said his friend kidnapped you."

Eliza kicked at a dirt clod as if it were Zeke's friend. "He grabbed me when Mother wasn't looking and pulled me onto his horse. We got all the way out here before that storm hit. It spooked the horse, and I escaped."

"Allan's looking for you," Jesse said.

Boone thought he could smell something sinister in the steam rising from a small hole in the ground near one of his hind legs. He tried to get a better whiff without calling attention to himself.

Eliza frowned. "Allan must be worried sick. That Zeke and his friends are gonna get it."

Jesse acted embarrassed, dragging a toe in the dirt. "You might not have to worry so much about Zeke no more."

Boone wriggled, trying to get his face closer to the hole, but suddenly he felt the ground shift beneath him. Eliza looked right at Boone's hiding place with a startled expression. Her eyes widened. Then the ground gave way, and Boone fell.

He opened his wings, trying to catch himself, but he only managed to bruise them as they flapped against rock and dirt. Then something looped around his face and arms. He struggled, and the grip on him got tighter. He realized the something was looped around his whole body. Panic surged through him. He fought, thrashing and fighting against the thing, but it only got tighter until it kept him from moving at all. He was hanging in midair in the dark, unable to move a muscle.

"Boone?" Jesse's voice came from above.

Out of the corner of one eye, Boone thought he saw Jesse's head peek over a hole about fifteen feet above him. It dripped with loose dirt and roots.

"Are you okay?" Jesse asked.

Boone wanted to snap that he was not okay, thank you very much, but he couldn't move his mouth. By the weak light coming in from the hole above, he could see that he hung suspended over an old mine shaft. He was caught in smelly, rotting rope, like a fly in a spider's web. He'd managed to drop Colorow's gun and—he realized with a sinking feeling—his hat.

When he tried to shift into human form to get untangled, waves of pain went through his body. He must have been injured in the fall.

"Don't worry," Jesse called. "I'll find another way in and get you down."

Jesse backed away from the giant hole in the ground behind the group of boulders. "A cave in," Eliza said, coming up behind him and staring at the hole.

"Probably gave way under Boone's weight," Jesse added. "Do you think there's another way in there?"

Eliza bit her lip. "This is the deserted mine Zeke's friend tried to drag me into. The entrance is this way."

She lit out across the meadow, skirting the hole by a wide margin. Jesse followed her. A stand of quaking aspen trees with half their leaves turned from green to yellow stood on the west end of the meadow. Among the trees, the ground slowly inclined until they came to a tall knoll. Eliza walked around it to a pile of wooden beams that covered an opening in the knoll. Jesse tried to shove one of the beams aside. Eliza bent down, and together they were able to heave the beam over to increase the opening enough for them to squeeze through.

Eliza shifted her feet, biting her lower lip again. "Deserted mines are dangerous. There's bad air, and cave ins." She winced.

Jesse felt a twinge of annoyance. He didn't get this girl at all. "Look, if you want to stay here, that's fine by me. But I need to go rescue my friend..." He stopped, marveling at that last word. It felt warm and soft on his tongue, like new honey. He jutted his chin out at her. "I'm going down there to help my friend. You do what you want."

He slithered into the hole and found himself in a tunnel. Several carts clustered to one side. They looked rusted in what little light came in from the entrance. Wooden beams held up the ceiling, spaced every ten feet or so, and marched off into the darkness in the direction of Boone's fall. Puddles of water pooled in low spots of the floor, covering up rusted cart tracks in several places.

"Ow!" There was the sound of cloth ripping, and Eliza stumbled into the tunnel next to Jesse. She frowned and fingered a tear in her skirt. "Mother will kill me," she mumbled.

"It's just clothes," Jesse said. He felt strangely pleased that she had chosen to come with him after all.

Jesse took the lead, walking into the tunnel. After a few steps, the light from the entrance faded. He slowed.

"I don't have a light on me."

"It's not that dark."

"Well, I can't see. Can you?"

"Perfectly!"

Eliza moved in front of him, grabbing his hand and pulling him after her. What an arrogant little thing she was! He wouldn't be surprised if she tripped over the cart track in the dark. There was no way she could see better than he could. She just wanted to be the one in charge.

Her hand felt warm and soft in his. His palm grew sweaty, and he wanted to yank away from her.

"I thought you were afraid of mines," Jesse said.

"Not afraid, exactly," Eliza said. She sounded more confident. "My papa taught me a lot about the earth. He knew the dangers of mining. There are lots of dangers, like poisonous gases, cave ins, and floods."

"Not to mention this 'widowmaker' everybody in town talks about," Jesse said.

He felt her stiffen. Her hand suddenly seemed like a wooden board.

"Those are just rumors. Normal mining accidents. That's all they are."

"Yeah. Silly to think somebody could have caused them." He felt Pa's harsh words ring in his ears. *There ain't no mortal man with that kind of power!* Jesse swallowed hard. "I guess mining's a dangerous undertaking anyhow."

Eliza let go of his hand and pointed ahead. He realized he could see her again, faintly.

"I think that's the 'back door' up ahead that your friend made."

After another minute of walking, they came to a larger chamber. A jagged hole in the ceiling showed glimpses of the sky and let in a feeble light. It wasn't enough to penetrate the circular shaft dropping away in front of them.

"There he is," Eliza said, pointing up.

Boone hung tangled in a mess of rope from a creaking beam jammed into the ceiling. It looked like a pulley system that once hauled a platform up and down the shaft like an elevator. The platform now lay in a broken heap of rotting wood off to one side of the shaft. Boone's red scales glittered in the wan light from the hole in the ceiling. He wriggled some, but couldn't seem to get free of the rope.

"What is he?" Eliza asked. Jesse was surprised she didn't show fear, only curiosity.

"Boone's a dragon," he said. He didn't know how else to describe the huge creature hanging above them, so he left it at that, and she seemed to accept it.

"He's gotten himself into quite a fix," Eliza said.

Jesse looked around for a way to reach Boone. He spotted a fallen beam half propped against the wall on top of a pile of rock.

He pulled his fishing knife out of its sheath. "Stay here," he told Eliza.

He hopped onto the beam and clambered up it before he could think too much about what he was doing. His boot heels clacked loudly on the wood.

As he got closer, Jesse could see Boone's big eye staring down at the shaft below in apparent fear. Boone wriggled harder.

"You keep that up and I'll never get you down," Jesse said. "Hold still."

Putting the knife between his teeth, Jesse grabbed on to a piece of rock jutting out from the wall and wedged a boot toe into a crevice.

Eliza gasped. "Be careful, Jesse!"

He tried to ignore the butterflies her concern created in his belly.

Inching his way up the wall, he got high enough to reach the ropes. He gripped a rock he hoped was secure and took the knife in his other hand. He wedged it under one of the rope strands and started sawing.

"I hope your scales are tough," he said. "'Cause this old knife is sharp."

After what seemed like forever, the rope finally broke and Jesse placed his knife under another strand. It took six broken strands before Boone was able to shake his muzzle free.

"You'd best hurry," Boone panted.

"I'm doing the best I can," Jesse said.

"Well, do it a mite faster. I can smell a basilisk in that shaft."

"A what?"

"A basilisk, something like a giant snake. Dragons and basilisks ain't exactly bosom pals. We need to get out of here pronto!"

Jesse sawed at another rope. "Okay, okay."

"Um, boys?" Eliza wasn't watching them anymore. Her eyes were glued on the mining shaft. "I think I saw something move down there."

"Don't look at it!" Boone said. "A basilisk can turn you to stone with its eyes."

Eliza quickly looked away from the shaft. The sagging skin around the eye of the ruined side of her face made her look frightened, much more frightened than she'd seemed of Boone.

"Hurry up!" Boone said.

"I am!" Jesse snapped. His grip on the rock holding him up grew slick with sweat. He sawed at the ropes faster, and Boone got one arm free. The beam from which Boone was suspended creaked and moaned ominously.

"The smell is getting stronger," Boone said. "I think that thing is headed this way."

Jesse spotted the main rope that led to a pulley above. If he could reach that, maybe he could get Boone free in a hurry.

"Girly," Boone said to Eliza, "move back—"

"My name isn't 'Girly,'" Eliza said, looking up at him and perching one hand on her hip. "It's Eliza."

Boone rolled one giant eye. "Whatever. Move back into the tunnel. If I have to spit fire at that basilisk, I don't want them pretty braids getting singed."

Eliza grew pale. She touched her hair. "Fire?"

Jesse reached for the main rope. He couldn't quite get it.

There was a low rumble coming from deep below. A tremor shook the ground, like a giant waking up. Eliza screamed.

Jesse's hand slipped on the rock support. With everything he had, he pushed off from the wall with his legs and leaped through space, aiming for the lead rope. Boone's head swiveled around in alarm. He saw Jesse's intent, and his eyes widened.

"No!" he yelled.

Jesse caught the lead rope with one hand and swung the knife with all his strength. The rope snapped under the pressure of the blade.

A roaring filled Jesse's ears as he fell. He was caught in a tangle of rope, dragon scales, and dirt. He flailed his arms, fighting, but he continued to fall. When he hit bottom, he gasped for breath like a land-bound fish. The ground under him heaved.

"Of all the block-headed, idiotic…" Boone spluttered. Jesse realized he was on top of Boone, but it was too dark to see anything. "Why'd you cut that rope?"

Jesse gasped for air and coughed. He bounced around as Boone wriggled under him. "I was trying…to get you free!"

"Well, it didn't work," Boone said.

Jesse wanted to cuss, but he remembered Eliza might hear him from up above.

"I lost my knife," he said instead.

"You're joshing me."

"Are you okay?" Eliza's voice came drifting down to them. It was faint and wreathed in echoes. Jesse thought he could make out her pale face peering over the edge above. At this distance, she looked normal, her disfigurement gone.

"How about finding that knife?" Boone said impatiently. "I'm still tied up in all this rope."

"Why don't you just change into a human?" Jesse asked.

"Because something got knocked sideways when I fell into this mess, and it'll hurt like the dickens if I shift right now," Boone snapped.

"Well, I can't see a dad-blasted thing down here!"

A glimmer of light caught Jesse's eye. A small glowing bubble drifted out of a side tunnel halfway up the shaft and lazily fell until it hovered over Jesse's head, lighting up the shaft around them.

"What's that?" he asked.

"Witchlight. You're a mage, remember?"

Jesse felt a prick of annoyance. "Is that supposed to mean something to me?"

Boone rolled his eyes. "You can summon light when you need it. There must have been a witchlight trapped in here. It came when you called. Now, how about that knife?"

"Right."

Jesse stopped studying the glimmer of light that hovered above his head and slid off Boone's belly, searching the mud on the ground.

The bottom of the shaft was just big enough that Boone could fit. His body was cramped up against one side, tangled worse than ever despite his muzzle remaining free. There were two paces open between Boone and the other shaft wall, just enough for Jesse to stand. A metal ladder was fastened to one side of the circular chamber. It looked like it went all the way to the top. Three dark openings spaced around the walls of the shaft looked like they led off into additional mining tunnels.

"Where are we, anyhow?" Jesse asked.

"Looks like a sump to me. It's used for collecting rainwater and the like." He wrinkled his nose. "Smells like a latrine. I hope my hat ain't down here. It'll need a major overhaul at the laundry after this."

"Why not just get a new one?"

"That hat ain't replaced so easy!" Boone said with a huff. "I had it made special in Philadelphia. It's got holes for my horns and everything."

Jesse held up his hands in a gesture of surrender. "Okay, okay." He spotted a glimmer of metal in the mud and dove for it. He came up with a rifle.

"Yours?" Jesse asked.

Boone grimaced. "A gun ain't gonna get the ropes off me."

Jesse tried to wipe the mud off the barrel with one sleeve. "Looks like a Springfield with a trapdoor. Impressive."

"It's dragon-made."

"Which means—?"

"It's got a magical kick to it. Look, that basilisk is still around somewheres, so if you could just find that knife—"

Jesse imagined a giant snake with venom dripping off its fangs, red eyes, and a rattle on its tail. Although a jab of fear went through his gut at the thought of facing such a creature, he also felt a morbid fascination with the idea of seeing it for real.

A steady ringing noise filled the sump, and the ladder shuddered. Jesse looked up to see Eliza climbing toward them, skirt tied up between her legs to keep her modest.

"Eliza, what are you doing?" he asked.

"You don't think I'll let you two have all the fun, do you?" she asked pertly. "Besides, I thought you might need this."

She hopped off the ladder, making a splash in the mud as she landed, and held out his knife.

"I don't even want to know what you just stepped in, Girly," Boone groaned.

With a cry, Jesse snatched up the knife. "Where was it?" he asked as he bent to the task of cutting the ropes off Boone.

"At the edge of one of those side tunnels," she said. "I could see it shining when that floating light came out of there."

"About time!" Boone said. He shook off the ropes and twisted around onto his hind legs. Jesse and Eliza moved back as far as they could to give him room. "Let's get out of here." Boone started to spread his wings, but then jerked to a stop with a cry.

Jesse thought one wing dangled at an unnatural angle. "Hang tight a second," he said.

He scrambled up the metal ladder high enough that he could get a good look at Boone's wings. One hung limp and crooked.

"Looks like it's broken," he said. "You want I should set it for you?"

"Have you ever set a broken limb afore?"

"Once. On a rabbit."

Boone snorted. "Shoot me now and get it over with."

"If we can't fly out of here," Eliza said, "we'll have to climb." She started up the ladder. "Coming, boys?"

Jesse watched as Boone transformed into a human. It was like wax melting in the sun, only instead of ending up in a puddle, the wax reshaped into the teenage boy Jesse was used to seeing, with the shadow of the dragon hovering around him and moving as he did.

"Wow!" Eliza said.

Boone's face was pinched and creased with pain. As soon as he'd finished transforming, he fell to the ground, cradled one arm in the other. The hurt arm was bent wrong in the middle.

"Ain't never transformed with a broke limb before," Boone panted.

"Can you climb?" Eliza asked.

Jesse helped Boone to his feet. Boone's jaw was clenched tight, his eyes shining with unshed tears. It was a moment before he answered, "I think so."

"You go first," Jesse said to Boone. "I'll carry the gun."

Boone nodded and started for the ladder, following Eliza. Jesse came last. It was slow going, as Boone could only use one arm. They hadn't gone far when Boone stopped suddenly, hissing.

"Your arm hurt?" Jesse asked with concern. "I hope you ain't about to swoon, because you're too big for me to catch."

"The smell!" Boone said, trying to bury his nose in his good shoulder. "It's getting stronger."

Now that Jesse had stopped climbing, he heard something slithering down the shaft.

"Don't look now, kids," Boone said, "but I think we got company."

In spite of the fear that gripped his insides, Jesse was curious to see what a basilisk looked like. And just like that, without any further thought, the witchlight that had been hovering around them zipped up the shaft.

"I told you not to look at it!" Boone yelled.

The witchlight went out immediately, plunging them into darkness, but not before Jesse caught a glimpse of what slithered down the ladder.

"A chicken?" he said.

"Well, what did you expect?" Boone asked.

"I thought you said it was a snake."

"The bottom half is a snake, and the top half is a rooster."

"Are all magical creatures freaks of nature?"

Boone growled low and deep. "That's an awful personal remark, Jesse Owens."

Eliza's voice sounded tense from above them. "Do you think you two could have your little chit-chat later? That thing is almost on top of us!"

"Right!" Jesse started up the ladder, and then realized he still had the rifle. "Hold on!" he said.

He threaded one arm through a ladder rung, keeping his balance while he brought the gun to his shoulder. He aimed just lower from where he had glimpsed the basilisk and away from Boone and Eliza on the ladder above, then squeezed the trigger. The gun kicked back into his shoulder, the sound echoing and ringing in his ears. There was a flash of light that lit up the shaft for a brief second. Jesse caught a glimpse of Eliza's face looking down at him. Both sides were smooth and clear. He blinked. The sudden light was playing tricks with his eyes.

"C'mon," Eliza yelled. She sounded on the verge of panic. "Let's get out of this sump. There's an opening to your right, Boone."

"To my right?"

Jesse heard a gasp of pain as the ladder creaked and shuddered. Boone must have jumped off.

There was a hiss from above, and suddenly Jesse felt a burning pain in one shoulder. He cried out.

"Jesse!" Eliza screamed.

Jesse clamped down on the pain with anger. He brought the gun back up, pointing lower than where he had last aimed, and fired. Again, the shaft was filled with a booming sound that set his ears ringing.

Sound came back slowly. When it did, he could hear Eliza screaming at him. "Jump, Jesse! Now!"

Without thinking too much about it, he pushed off from the ladder, jumping up and flailing with one arm. He didn't know how he managed to catch the ledge in his hand. It was almost as if the ledge grabbed for him. Then Eliza's cold fingers gripped his wrist, and she was tugging at him. He scrabbled on the wall of the sump with his boots and found several toe holds he used to push himself up and over the ledge.

When he got up, she didn't let him rest. She grabbed his hand and hauled him forward.

"Where are we going?" Jesse asked breathlessly.

"This is a stope," Eliza said. "A tunnel they dug off the main shaft to follow a vein of ore."

"Let's just hope it don't lead to a dead end," Boone said. His voice was strained, and he sounded out of breath.

Jesse stubbed a toe on an outcropping of rock. He stumbled and fell to his knees.

"Jesse!" Eliza said.

"We gotta hurry!" Boone urged.

Jesse felt frustration and anger overpowering him. His foot throbbed. The gun felt heavy in his hands. "Why does it have to be so confounded dark?" he yelled.

When he said the last word, a rumble shook the ground, and six witchlights popped into existence around his head. The stope was suddenly flooded with light.

There was a hiss behind them. They all turned automatically to look.

The basilisk was at the stope's entrance, shying away from the light. It had dark scales that glistened in the witchlight. The lower body of a snake as thick around as a man coiled and flexed. Halfway up, black feathers overlapped the scales, covering stubby wings and a huge chicken head. The feathers shimmered as if they were made of the same material as the scales. The chicken half flapped its wings and clacked its beak in agitation. It was wearing a tan hat at a cocky angle.

"That piece of mule hide is wearing my hat!" Boone yelled.

"I'll buy you a new one," Eliza said. She grabbed Jesse's hand and Boone's good arm and hauled them down the stope at a dead run.

A stream of liquid shot past their heads and hit the wall of the stope. They stumbled away from it.

"Look out!" Boone yelled. "It's spitting acid."

Jesse was tired of this cat-and-mouse game. He skidded to a stop, pulling away from Eliza. She stopped and stared back at him.

"What are you doing, Jesse?"

Squeezing his eyes shut, he spun around in one smooth motion, pulling the gun up to his shoulder.

"Aim for the eyes," Boone panted. "Guns ain't no good against the scales, or even most of the feathers.'

"Got it."

Jesse tilted the gun up slightly, hoping it was aimed at the basilisk's head. He squeezed the trigger. He thought he heard a high-pitched squeal just before the gun's report set his ears ringing.

Jesse risked cracking his eyes open to see if he'd hit anything. The basilisk wasn't far away, rearing back with a bloody scratch along the side of its face. Jesse felt a crushing disappointment. He'd only grazed it. But then he felt a rumbling under his feet. There was a whoosh of air from the stope opening, and a wave of heat following it.

"Oh, no."

A huge ball of crackling lightning formed and raced toward them.

"Run!" he screamed at his friends. "Run!"

Chapter 19
A Female Will Put Flavor in Your Grub

J esse turned and ran for all he was worth. The cry of the
basilisk was dull to his ears after the deafening retort of
the gun, but he knew the creature was racing after him.
Jesse caught up with Boone and Eliza and swept one arm
around Boone while Eliza gripped Boone's other side. The
three of them raced down the stope as fast as they could.

The whole time, Jesse couldn't get the image of the
frozen chicken coop out of his head. He never should have
tried to use a gun again. Only this time, instead of ice, he
had somehow managed to call up a ball made of lightning,
and he and his friends were about to get sizzled by it.

"A cave in!" Boone yelled. "We're trapped!"

Sure enough, the dancing witchlights spinning furiously
around Jesse's head illuminated a mess of boulders and
broken beams that blocked their escape. Boone and Jesse
stumbled to a halt, but Eliza kept going until she nearly ran
into the obstacle. She slapped one hand against a rock. With

the other, she traced a curved line that doubled back on itself and ended with a dot. It glowed a bright yellow, and the rock seemed to turn to mud under her hands. She pushed it aside as easily as if it were made of bread dough, making an opening large enough for them to get through. The basilisk was coming up right behind them.

Jesse grabbed Boone's collar and pulled him toward the opening. Just before they slipped through, Boone spun, and with a scream of agony, snatched his hat from the basilisk's head.

Then they were falling through the opening. Eliza dove after them, her hands working furiously to close the gap. Jesse could see the midsection of the basilisk through the opening. It tried to push forward, to get its head through. It squawked like a regular chicken. Then there was a crackling sound, and the basilisk screeched. Jesse saw light envelop it just as Eliza covered the last part of the opening.

She cried out in pain and fell to the ground, cradling her hands.

Jesse sprang forward. "What happened?"

She was sobbing, tears marring two smooth cheeks. She held up her palms to him. They were red and starting to swell.

Jesse cussed under his breath. "I'm sorry, Eliza. It's all my fault!" He kicked at a nearby rock to vent his anger at himself. "I am such an idiot! I'm so sorry!"

"She can heal it," Boone said quietly.

Jesse turned to stare at Boone. Boone stood behind them, cradling his broken arm, glaring at Eliza.

"What do you mean?" Jesse asked.

"She can heal it," Boone repeated. "Can't you, Girly." It wasn't a question.

Eliza swiped at her tears with her upper arms. "It still hurts!" She looked down at her hands. Before Jesse's eyes, the redness and swelling disappeared.

It was then that Jesse registered that the scars on her face were gone. Her skin was smooth, and the droopiness around the left eye had disappeared. Her face was symmetrical again. She was beautiful.

"Why didn't you tell me you're a…a…" The word escaped his memory.

"A mage," Boone said. "To be exact, a terramage."

"Yes!" Jesse said. A surge of elation rose in him. "Like me!"

"Excepting she's had a bit of training, though I can't figure where. I ain't never seen her in the Veiled Canyon, and I've been there a long time."

"Papa taught me," Eliza said, a look of defiance in her eyes.

"Your papa was a mage?" Boone asked.

"A Katsina."

Boone seemed shocked. "A Katsina? Then you're... he's...you mean..." He rubbed a hand against his broken arm and winced. "He was...stationed here. To guard the mountains and the pot shard. Wasn't he?"

Jesse looked from Boone to Eliza. Eliza seemed to know exactly what Boone meant. "What pot shard?" Jesse asked. "What do you mean, 'stationed here'?"

Eliza looked steadily up at Boone. "He was faithful in maintaining his post until he disappeared five months ago. Now I guard the mountains."

Boone's face grew pinched and angry. "Or you hunt for the pot shard. Tell me the truth—ain't you the one who's been causing all these mining accidents? You're looking for the shard, ain't you?"

"What are you talking about?" Jesse demanded. He felt a need to stand up for Eliza against Boone's accusations.

Boone jabbed a finger toward Eliza. "Her," he said. "She's the widowmaker!"

Boone couldn't believe he'd been such an idiot! All this time, the widowmaker was right under his nose at Mrs. Matthews' house. He'd even smelled this girl working magic with his own nose and failed to recognize her later under the guise of her burned face.

But when he realized she could see in the dark, he began to understand the truth. Then it was confirmed as her disguise fell away during their flight from the basilisk, and he recognized the girl who had gotten him out of the trap at the Ulay.

His arm hurt something fierce and all he wanted to do was lie down and take a nap, but he forced himself to think.

Only a trained mage could have moved the rock as Eliza did, a mage with a great deal of power. She was young, but if she was telling the truth about her father being a Katsina, she'd had plenty of time to be trained in using glyphs to work magic. What Boone couldn't figure was how she could betray her father like this.

Jesse wrapped his arms around himself. His expression looked miserable as he spoke to Eliza. "You're the widowmaker?"

Eliza blinked back tears. "I didn't cause those accidents." She reached out toward Jesse, but he stepped away from her until his back hit the wall of the tunnel. One by one, the witchlights around him went out until there was only one left, bobbing slowly above his head.

Swiping at her tears with the back of her hand, Eliza turned to glare up at Boone. "Why do you think no one was killed in all those mining accidents?" she asked. "I was protecting them. Didn't I save you when you were trapped in the Ulay?"

Boone set his mouth and didn't answer. His arm sent waves of pain up through his shoulder and neck.

"Soon after Papa disappeared, accidents started happening," Eliza continued. "I knew it was magic, that someone was hunting for the pot shard. They didn't care if the miners got hurt; in fact, I imagine they were trying to scare everybody out of the mines so they could search more freely."

"What is this pot shard?" Jesse asked quietly.

"The Wité Pot," Boone said. "It was used by an evil mage named Orendos over two hundred years ago. He trapped the power of other mages with it so he could use their magic for himself. When the Katsina defeated Orendos, they broke the pot into pieces and hid them."

"Papa was left to protect these mountains and the hiding place of a shard," Eliza said.

"Where is your father now?" Boone asked.

She dropped her eyes. "I don't know. Allan and I searched for him last summer in the lowlands, but we never found him."

"He didn't die of a fever," Jesse said. His tone was cold, hard. "Like you told me."

"No. But I couldn't very well tell you the truth, could I, Jesse?"

"Why not? That's what friends do, ain't it? Oh, wait." He sneered at her. "You ain't my friend no more, are you?"

Eliza's lip started to tremble. She bit it, eyes swimming in tears as she looked at Jesse. When she spoke, her voice was thick with emotion. "I knew you were a mage from the minute I saw you, Jesse. I wanted to be your friend, but Allan said it was too dangerous. We don't know who's causing these accidents, and Allan thought it was you."

"How did you know I was a mage?"

"I can see sparks around you, especially when you're upset...like now."

Jesse scowled at her, but his eyes flicked to the air around him, as if he were trying to see the sparks.

"And I reckon you can see my true form," Boone said.

"My papa told me about dragons, but I never saw one before now. I just...I didn't know who to trust."

"That's smart, since a skinwalker could be anybody."

Eliza grew pale. "A skinwalker? Here?"

227

"That's what Colorow thought. He said it could be anyone. Even Jesse. Even you."

Jesse looked sharply at Boone. "I thought you said I was a thundermage."

"Unless you're masquerading as one because you're really an evil skinwalker fixing to collect the pieces of the Wité Pot and become the next Orendos."

"What?" Jesse's fists tightened into hard knots.

Boone was afraid he was about to get punched. He held up his good arm. "Relax, Jesse. I don't believe that no more. I'm willing to trust that you're no skinwalker."

Eliza stood up slowly, her chin rising. She looked like a young Katsina with her dark skin, square jaw, and her hair braided back. She smelled like one too, the acidic hint of magic hovering around her like a cloud. Boone marveled that he hadn't noticed it before.

"Believe that I'm no skinwalker either," Eliza said.

Boone studied her for several long moments in silence. He wished that his sense of smell could tell him whether someone was lying or not. His arm throbbed and made it hard to think. If Colorow were here, maybe he could figure this out.

Finally, Jesse said. "I believe her, Boone. I think we can trust her."

Boone continued to hesitate.

"If you don't believe what I say," Eliza went on, "then believe what I do. I saved you from the Ulay, didn't I? And here, underground, I have certain powers. I can help you again."

She stepped forward and Boone flinched, but she merely laid a cold hand on his broken arm. Even the light amount of pressure she placed on it made intense pain shoot up his arm. He sucked in his breath sharply.

Eliza kept her hand in place. She closed her eyes, and the smell of magic got stronger. He had smelled this before, in the Ulay. A warmth blossomed under her hand, getting warmer and warmer until the heat was almost unbearable. He growled in an effort to control the pain.

Eliza cried out and collapsed in a faint. Jesse dove forward, catching her just before her head hit the ground.

"What happened?" Jesse asked angrily.

Boone stared at his arm. He flexed the fingers and slowly rotated his shoulder in a circle. The pain was gone. "She healed it! And she didn't even use a glyph. How did she do that?" He noticed her eyes fluttering open. "How did you do that?" he demanded.

"Give her a minute," Jesse said.

Boone crouched beside Eliza, watching her as she recovered. "I reckon she's doing magic too strong for her.

She fainted before when she moved the rock to get me out of the Ulay."

Jesse looked up at Boone. "Glyphs are them writings you showed me, right?"

"The Katsina use dragon writing, or glyphs, to channel and focus their magic power. I ain't never seen human magic work that way, without glyphs."

Jesse's eyes shifted, looking beyond Boone. "Speaking of glyphs," Jesse said, "what do you reckon those are?"

Boone turned around, looking for what Jesse saw. On the ceiling above his head, a shape glowed, the light beginning to fade from it. He realized with a start that it was a petroglyph, much like the ones Madge had shown them in the treasure chamber.

Boone snatched the hat off his head, fishing in the inner band for his papers. The light of the petroglyph was fading fast. Soon it would disappear into the dark of the rock. He tore off an unused corner from one of the sheets and placed it against the rock, over the petroglyphs. "Quick! You got something to write with?"

Eliza opened her eyes. She reached out and picked up a rock. When she touched it, a flash of light lit the chamber for a moment. She handed it to Jesse, and he passed it on to Boone.

Boone turned the rock over in his hand. It was no longer a rock. Now it was a lump of charcoal.

"How'd you do that?" he asked Eliza as he rubbed the charcoal carefully across the paper, bringing out the etched symbols beneath it just before the light faded from them completely and they were no longer visible. To the left was the now-familiar shape of the pig nose that meant the Wité Pot, and to the right, a circle like a head with horns coming out the sides. "You don't need a glyph?"

Eliza pushed away from Jesse into a sitting position. She looked tired, but didn't seem in danger of fainting again.

"Some things I can do without glyphs. I'm a strong terramage."

"What's a terramage?" Jesse asked.

"That means I control the earth. I can mold it to my needs and shape it like clay. I can do the same thing with people."

"Like your face?" Jesse asked. "You can fix it?"

Eliza's expression became wistful. "It doesn't work on me. My face only looks like this when I'm underground. Up there, I look like a monster again."

"You ain't no monster," Jesse said quietly.

"Didn't your pa try to heal you?" Boone asked. "You said he was a Katsina."

"Of course he tried, but even he couldn't heal my skin where the fire burned me. That fire is the reason I have magic."

Jesse's expression brightened. "You said your pa taught you. Did he teach you how to interpret the Katsina writing?"

"Some," Eliza said hesitantly. "Dragon glyphs are complicated."

Boone felt a spark of excitement as he understood what Jesse was driving at. He thrust his papers at Eliza. "You think you can figure out what these mean?"

She took the papers from him, frowning at them.

"This sheet here," Boone said, "is what me and Colorow found in the Ulay. These glyphs on this other sheet were in a cave somewhere hereabouts." To Boone's relief, she didn't seem to notice his vague reference to Madge's treasure cave.

"I need more light," Eliza mumbled.

The witchlight drifted down until it hovered over her paper. She flashed a smile up at Jesse before returning to her study.

Finally, she took a deep breath. "This might not be exactly right," she said.

"It's okay," Boone said quickly. "Even if it's close, it'll be a sight more than I can read."

"I recognize this symbol here," she said, pointing to the shape of the headless man. "It indicates punishment. He's holding a head with horns that are bound together. That means trapped—magic power that's trapped."

"Colorow said that's the symbol for Orendos."

Eliza slowly nodded. "That makes sense. But why is his other arm stretched out?"

"Because he was stopped?" Jesse suggested.

"I don't know. This symbol here," Eliza pointed to the upside-down triangle. "It looks like the body of another person, but it doesn't seem complete."

Boone shifted around until he was peering over her shoulder. "That's what Jesse thought, but we couldn't figure what it means."

"What's that drawing on the other side of the paper?" Jesse asked, pointing to the sheet with the red background.

Eliza turned it over as Boone replied, "Oh, that's the map Colorow made of where the mining accidents happened."

Eliza looked up sharply at him. "A map?"

Boone shrugged. "It was the only paper I had on me in the Ulay."

"A map!" Eliza smiled. "You're a genius, Boone!"

"Huh?"

She flipped the paper back around to the rubbings. "That circle with the dots inside it is on all these papers."

"You mean the pig nose?" Boone asked.

Jesse tried to squelch a laugh and failed miserably. Boone shrugged with an apologetic smile.

"If we line up that symbol on each paper..." Eliza placed one paper over the other until all three were stacked. She held them up so that the witchlight was behind them. "It looks just like a map! The whole thing is a map."

"But I found them symbols in three totally different places," Boone protested.

"Isn't your pig nose the symbol for the Wité Pot?" Eliza asked with a smirk.

Boone felt himself flush. She had been listening. "Yeah, I reckon."

"Well, I bet this is a map to where the pot shard is hidden!"

Jesse came around behind her, next to Boone, looking over her other shoulder.

"Hey!" Boone said, his own excitement growing. "When you put the papers together like that, some of them symbols change. Orendos has a head now, and so does that triangle. The circle I just copied down makes it into a person!" He pointed to a third person who was now placed to the right of the other two. The head with horns lined up with the upside-down triangle body. "And all these lines up here connect now. They look like roads or paths."

"Or rivers," Jesse added. "This here big circle with the bunch of little dots inside—could that be Crystal Lake? Don't it got a river feeding it from the west and one going out on the south, just like this drawing?"

"I think you're right!" Eliza said. "The symbol for a river is a double zigzag, just like what's now on top of those lines. And look at these three double circles. The inside circles are filled. If I remember right, that means there's something hidden underground, maybe a mine or an underground cave, since this map is probably lots older than the mining operations in this area."

"What's with the double-headed snake thing next to that circle?" Boone asked, pointing to the upper right corner of the map.

Eliza frowned. "Danger. That means danger."

"Like a basilisk lair?" Boone asked.

"Maybe."

Jesse swallowed. "So this circle could be the cave system we're in right now."

Eliza looked up at him, her eyes wide.

Boone hardly dared breathe. With a shaking finger, he traced a path of lines to a symbol he knew on the left of the map. "I know what this is. It's a cliff dwelling. Looks like it's above the lake, but I don't recollect seeing any cliff dwellings in these here parts."

Eliza shook her head. "There aren't. At least, I haven't ever seen any, and Papa never said anything about one around here."

"Don't mean it ain't there, though," Boone said, thinking of Vihala's room in the Veiled Canyon and the magic hiding it from view.

"There's another of them circles under it," said Jesse. "Boone, just where do you reckon that treasure cave was that Madge showed us?"

Boone felt his stomach drop into his toes as a rush of cold went through him. "Couldn't have been far from there. You don't think...I mean...that treasure cave. Could that be where the shard was hidden all along? Maybe Madge touched some of that treasure after all."

Jesse's jaw firmed, a hardness entering his eyes. "I reckon there's only one way to find out."

Chapter 20
Waltzing Into a Bear Trap

Jesse suddenly wished he still had the gun, but he'd dropped it in their escape from the basilisk.

"So, you want to just go traipsing off through these tunnels, following the map?" Eliza asked, staring at Jesse incredulously.

Boone swiped his hat off the floor. He sniffed it and grimaced. "You got a better idea for getting out of here? I don't see no exits."

Eliza huffed. "You're crazy. You're both crazy. You want to go looking for the Wité Pot shard in some mysterious treasure cave when there's probably a...a *skinwalker* after it?"

Hearing Eliza call him crazy stung Jesse's feelings just a little, even though he'd labeled himself that more than once over the last few months.

"You don't have to come, Girly," Boone said with a grin. He held out a hand to her. "But I'll be taking my map back."

Eliza frowned at his hand and shoved the papers behind her back. "How are you going to read it? You two won't last more than five minutes without me. You'll get yourselves lost forever in this underground labyrinth."

Jesse didn't know what a labyrinth was, but he jumped on something else she'd said. "Then come with us," he urged. "We can't leave you down here by yourself anyhow."

"I can look after myself just fine," she retorted. "Especially underground."

She climbed to her feet and brushed off her petticoats, then turned on a boot heel and marched down the passage, head held high.

After a few steps, she stopped and glared back over her shoulder at them. "Well? Are you coming or not?"

Jesse jumped forward and hurried to catch up with her. Boone moved more slowly, shaking his head and muttering about confounded females.

They walked for what seemed like hours, stopping every time they came to a crossroads for Eliza to consult the map. The tunnels were unlike those Jesse had seen in the abandoned mine or the Bellawest. There were no beams to support the ceiling, lanterns hanging from the walls, or cart tracks on the floor. They twisted and curved through a naturally formed cave system, following a path that was sometimes narrow, sometimes wide until Jesse was no longer sure from which direction they'd started.

The only light was the witchlight that continued to follow Jesse, giving a wan glow to the deep darkness that seemed to push in on every side. Jesse felt the oppression of it, and after a while tried to summon another witchlight to dispel more of the gloom. It didn't come.

"The air is stale in here," Eliza remarked after leading them to the left at a crossroads. "I hope we don't run into any poisonous gas."

"How will we know?" Jesse asked.

"Miners take a caged canary into the mine with them. If the canary faints, they know the air is bad."

"We don't have a canary. All we've got is a dragon."

Boone snorted from where he walked behind them. "I resemble that remark," he said.

"Do you think that's what happened to your pa?" Jesse asked. "That he ran into some bad air or something underground?"

Eliza's smile faded. "No. The tommyknockers would have warned him of danger underground."

"Tommyknockers?" Boone said scornfully. "Colorow disappeared right after we heard a tommyknocker. I ain't so sure I trust the little beggars."

Jesse felt the familiar flush of embarrassment when Eliza and Boone discussed something that he'd never heard of from this new world of magic. "I don't suppose you want to explain what tommyknockers are?"

"Little men," Boone said.

Eliza threw a frown at Boone over her shoulder. "They warn people about disasters underground. Mining isn't exactly a safe occupation. There are cave ins, tremors, poisonous gasses. Tommyknockers know when bad things are going to happen. They use little metal hammers to tap on the walls and warn people so they can get out safely."

"Are you sure that's what the hammers are for?" Boone asked. "Maybe they use them to lure somebody to come looking and then they use them hammers to knock folks upside the head."

Eliza stopped and rounded on Boone, one hand flying to her hip. "Do you really think that's what happened to your friend?"

Boone's grin slipped. "I reckon not. He was a Katsina, like your pa. He wouldn't fall for such shenanigans."

"I don't suppose he would."

They resumed walking.

"So, we have two Katsina missing," Jesse said slowly. "Do you think that's important?"

"I think it means something mighty dangerous is out there," Boone said, his voice low and soft. "We'd best watch where we step."

"Speaking of which," Eliza said as they came to another branching corridor. She pulled out the map. "If I decipher this right, I think that tunnel to the left might lead to the Bellawest. We could get out of here now, then fetch Allan and maybe the sheriff before we investigate this treasure cave you boys were talking about."

Jesse wasn't so sure about Allan, but he'd like to fetch Pa. It would be a great relief to tell Pa everything he'd learned since running away in the storm and turn the whole search for this what's-it pot and the skinwalker over to Pa and Sam and the adults.

"We might run into a dead end," Boone said, pointing to the short line on the map she proposed to follow.

Eliza shrugged. "We could always turn around if that happens."

Jesse thought he heard something coming from the tunnel on the left.

"But what if the skinwalker is there, right now, stealing the pot shard?" Boone argued. "We'd catch her in the act. If we come back later, she'll be gone."

Jesse took a few tentative steps into the left tunnel.

"I thought you said she's already taken it," Eliza snapped.

"Madge just showed us the treasure room. We don't know if the pot shard was missing or not," Boone said.

Jesse took several more steps until the sound got stronger and he was sure he recognized it.

Eliza continued to argue with Boone. "We don't know if she's there right now, either,"

"Exactly! We gotta get there and find out before it's too late."

"It may already be too late."

"Hey!" Jesse interrupted, spinning back to them with excitement. "I think I hear Rio!"

Boone frowned. "Not that smelly animal again."

"Listen!" Jesse said.

They all three fell silent until the unmistakable echo of a horse's whinnying could be heard drifting from the tunnel on the left.

"We left him at the entrance to the Bellawest, remember, Boone? I think Eliza's right. I think this tunnel does connect to the Bellawest."

A smug expression lit up Eliza's face.

Boone looked from one to the other of them, his expression falling into a glower. "Fine. We'll fetch help. But don't blame me if the skinwalker gets away!"

With a nod of satisfaction, Eliza strode forward, leading the way past Jesse down the new corridor. She hadn't gone more than five steps when an echoing tap filled the tunnel, like metal ringing on the rock. They all stopped, turning to stare at each other with mixed emotions on their faces as the tap repeated twice before falling into silence.

"Tommyknocker!" Boone hissed.

Suddenly, a rumbling filled the tunnel and the ground opened up beneath Eliza's feet. She fell with a sharp scream.

Jesse hesitated in shock for just a moment. In that moment, the ground closed back up, the hole disappearing. Leaping into action, Jesse raced forward with Boone. Jesse crashed to his knees, feeling the ground where Eliza had disappeared. It was as solid as the rest of the tunnel around them, rough, unyielding rock that cut his hands as he frantically searched for the hole she had fallen into. At last he was forced to admit it. Eliza was gone.

"What happened?" Jesse yelled.

"I don't know!" Boone yelled back. He felt helpless. The girl had fallen through a hole in the ground that had closed right up over her head. Is that what had happened to Colorow? Frustrated, Boone stomped on the ground where she'd disappeared, stronger and stronger stomps that shook the tunnel. He didn't care if he brought the ceiling down on his fool head.

Jesse still sat on the ground, a stricken look on his face. "She couldn't have just disappeared," he said.

"Well, she did!" Boone stopped slamming his foot against the ground as an idea occurred to him. He narrowed his eyes suspiciously. "The tommyknocker," he said.

"What?"

"Sneaking little…"

Jesse scrambled back frantically as Boone suddenly transformed. It was a tight squeeze, and Boone remembered why he didn't like underground spaces. He swallowed his claustrophobia and swiveled his head around, flicking his tongue out to track the scent. There—the hint of mushrooms and sulfur coming from the main tunnel.

He shifted back into his human form, taking a deep breath now that his lungs could expand. "This way," he said, running past Jesse. He stopped when he realized Jesse wasn't following. "You coming?"

Jesse still sat on his rump in the side tunnel. Boone nearly burst out laughing at the shocked look on his face. "What?" Boone said with a shrug. "I don't pick up smells nearly so good when I'm human. We'd best hurry. That little beggar will be getting away right quick now that he's given his so-called *warning*."

Scrambling to his feet, Jesse brushed dirt off his trousers. "Who?"

Boone's answer came out with a growl. "That tommyknocker."

Eliza had the map when she disappeared, but Boone figured they didn't need it anymore. Now he'd identified the tommyknocker's smell, he was able to follow it deeper into the tunnels, even with his human nose. He felt a twinge of satisfaction when the course led them toward Madge's treasure again, but sobered when he thought of what had happened to Eliza. True, the girl could be a regular pain in the neck, but he kind of liked her spunk all the same. He hoped she was okay, wherever she'd gone.

Boone and Jesse were moving so fast that Boone almost missed it when he lost the scent. He abruptly came to a stop and Jesse ran into him, nearly knocking them both to the ground.

"Watch it!" Boone said.

"If you'd give me a warning, I would," Jesse grumped back.

Boone took a deep whiff of the air. The only way to be sure the scent was gone was to shift to his dragon form, but the tunnel had gotten smaller and he didn't think he would fit anymore. He turned around and took a few steps back, still sniffing.

"You lost the scent?" Jesse asked. "Great! Now what?"

Boone retraced their steps, taking in deep breaths through his nose. The air in the tunnel was stale and flat, so it was easy to spot the tang of sulfur when it began to tickle his nose. There was an alcove to the left that they'd missed in their headlong pursuit of the tommyknocker.

It looked as if someone had started to create a branching tunnel and then a cave in had stopped the work before it had really begun. The alcove was dark, a good five strides long before it ended in a huge angular slab of rock that slanted down from the ceiling to the floor. Boone took a whiff, then another. A slow smile crept over his face. "Gotcha!" he whispered.

Boone pounced, using all his strength to tackle what looked like empty air just a step or two inside the alcove.

There was a high-pitched squawk, and suddenly Boone was grappling with a little man. He was wiry and no taller than Boone's waist. He had black hair and a long beard that looked like a bunch of dark grapes hung on a thin, narrow face. Red veins under his blue skin stood out like lines on a map, and his arms bulged absurdly as he struggled with Boone. He swung around a silver hammer almost bigger than he was tall and rapped Boone smartly on the knuckles.

Boone cried out in pain, his hand shooting to his mouth for comfort. In that moment, the tommyknocker slipped away. He didn't get far. At the mouth of the alcove, Jesse threw himself at the little man, grabbing him around the waist and pulling them both to the ground. Before the tommyknocker could react, Jesse wrapped one arm around his neck, putting him into a headlock and twisting the arm with the hammer up behind him.

"Let me go!" the tommyknocker cried in a wispy voice like the buzzing of a wasp. "Let me go!"

Boone panted, shaking his injured hand. He glared. "Not until you tell us what happened to our friend," he growled.

The tommyknocker stopped struggling and looked up at Boone with sunken eyes that nearly disappeared as they narrowed. "How should I know?"

Boone crouched on the ground and brought his face inches from the tommyknocker's. "I ain't in the mood for games," he said in a low and menacing voice. "You know what I am?"

The color drained out of the tommyknocker's face until the blue skin was nearly white. His orange-colored lips stood out starkly, pursed into a thin line.

"I could chew you up for breakfast and spit you out before you could say boo," Boone continued.

"Ain't no call for violence, Boone," Jesse said in a calm tone that belied the wrestler's hold he had on the tommyknocker. "I'm sure this critter will tell us what we need to know. So, where is Eliza?"

The tommyknocker struggled against Jesse's grip a moment longer, then sagged when he seemed to realize he couldn't get free. "You let me go, I take you to the girl," he said.

"We let you go, you disappear," Boone said. "I ain't falling for your tricks."

"What are you afraid of, dragon? You'll just sniff me down, like you did before."

Jesse glanced at Boone, then back at the little man. "If I let go, you'll take us to Eliza?" he asked.

"On my honor," the tommyknocker said.

"Which I don't trust as far as I can throw you," Boone growled.

"Trust me or not, but it's the only way you'll find your friend again," the tommyknocker said, lips curving into an evil-looking smile.

Boone shook his head at Jesse, but he could tell Jesse was ready to believe the evil little cockroach.

"You can eat him for breakfast if he tries anything funny," Jesse said as he slowly moved his arms and let the tommyknocker go.

He eyed them both as he carefully climbed to his feet, slowly pointing up at the ceiling.

Boone narrowed his eyes, suspecting some sort of trick, but he looked up when Jesse gasped.

The ceiling shimmered. What was solid rock was replaced by an opening, a crack that ran the length of the alcove and widened above the rock slab. It looked like they could reach it if they climbed up the slab, though the opening was still narrow.

"Climb the ladder all the way to the top," the tommyknocker said, flashing that evil grin.

Boone groaned and rolled his eyes. The tommyknocker had probably made the opening small on purpose. Boone considered eating the little devil, but decided he would taste bitter.

"You want us to go up there?" Jesse asked.

The little man rubbed his hands together. "Only if you want to see your friend again."

Jesse still couldn't get over the way the cleft had appeared in what had been solid rock a moment before. The crack looked just big enough to scrape through if they held their breath. He thought about the opening between the tree roots where he and Boone had followed Madge into the treasure cave earlier that week. Why were all underground spaces so narrow?

"Just climb up the rock," the tommyknocker said, "and through that crevice. There'll be a ladder. Go to the top, and you'll find her."

"You know we're fools for doing this," Boone hissed close to Jesse's ear.

"I know."

Jesse wished more than ever that he still had the cold, hard steel of the gun between his fingers. Taking a deep breath, he scrambled up the slab of rock. His boots slipped on the smooth surface, but he found enough purchase that he was able to get up to the level of the ceiling and grab the edges of the crevice. With a grunt, he heaved himself up through it. The edges scraped his arms and back, but he was able to get through.

"What's up there?" Boone's voice echoed from below as Jesse's witchlight came through the crack and bobbed around his head.

Jesse took a minute to study his surroundings before he answered. He was in a small, round chamber that rose into the darkness, much like the basilisk's sump, only this was much smaller and a natural formation rather than man-made. It reminded Jesse of being inside the chimney of a house.

In front of him, he could see a narrow slit opening into another chamber. He stepped up to it and sent the witchlight through with a thought, marveling at how easy it was to control the little things. The light revealed Madge's treasure chamber. The jewels and coins winked with glares that seemed sinister, after Boone's talk of a skinwalker. From Jesse's vantage point, he figured he was peering out from a hidden opening behind the panel where they had seen the petroglyphs.

Jesse spotted something several steps into the room on a pile of wooden boxes. It glinted, partly hidden by an animal skin he didn't recognize. He walked into the chamber to get a better look. Hesitating, he remembered what Madge had said about the treasure being cursed. But she was just a crazy old coot, wasn't she? It wouldn't really be cursed, unless Boone was right and that pot shard was hidden here.

Making up his mind, Jesse grabbed the animal skin and pulled it away. Underneath it was a handgun—at least, he thought it was. It was fashioned differently from any pistol he'd ever seen. A long, thin barrel that looked like it might be made of copper gleamed in the witchlight. Jesse could see several dragon glyphs running all along the barrel. At one end of the gun, loops and coils of silver and gold were intricately woven together, like clockwork. The handle was made of smooth, rose-colored wood, shaped in the head of a bird that had a small glittering diamond for an eye.

"Jesse?" Boone's voice was muffled.

Jesse grabbed the strange gun and shoved it under his belt, then returned to the hidden chamber. This time, he noticed a wooden ladder bound together with rough rope that ascended up into darkness.

"Looks like it keeps going up," Jesse called down to Boone.

"Hang on," Boone replied. "I'm coming."

Jesse heard boot heels scraping against rock and dirt tumbling down, followed by cussing. Finally, Boone's hat rose through the opening. It looked more battered than when Jesse had first met Boone. Now several dark streaks marred the smooth leather, and it was slightly squashed on the crown. Boone's head followed the hat, his face pinched into a frown.

"Dang opening's too small," he said.

He grunted as he tried to squeeze up through the slit. Jesse grabbed his arm and helped pull him through.

"I ever tell you how much I hate underground spaces?" Boone said as he got his waist above the hole and pulled one leg through.

Jesse tried to see beyond Boone. "Is that tommyknocker coming?"

Boone scowled. "He up and disappeared as soon as I started climbing. I tell you, Jesse, this seems mighty fishy to me. Maybe we should just get on out of here."

"Madge's treasure is just on the other side of this wall," Jesse said. "You think we should look for the pot shard?"

Boone perched on the lip of the crevice and licked his lips. He looked at the wall, then up at the chimney. He seemed torn by indecision, but he said, "I reckon finding Eliza's more important than the shard."

"The tommyknocker said we should go all the way up. That ladder don't hardly look like it'll hold us, though."

Boone took off his hat, ran a hand through his hair, and put the hat back on. "It's like them ladders back home in the Veiled Canyon. They're stronger than you think."

Jesse was the first to start climbing. They went up for about thirty feet, the ladder creaking ominously under their weight. Jesse tried not to picture what would happen if the old wood broke.

"You had that tommyknocker in a pretty good headlock," Boone panted when they were more than halfway up. "How'd you learn to wrestle like that?"

"I got an older brother," Jesse said. "Simple as that." If they got into a match now, Jesse didn't think Sam would fare as well as he had before moving to Colorado.

"Well, I'm mighty glad you got a grip on that slippery little devil," Boone said.

Jesse looked up at the remainder of the ladder. The witchlight bobbed above his head, but there was another light coming from above. "You may not thank me when all's said and done," Jesse said. "I reckon we're about to find a heap of trouble."

When Jesse reached the top, he was able to step off the ladder onto a rock shelf. Above, the chimney narrowed to an impassable shaft, continuing on for another forty feet where it opened to a small patch of gray sky. It felt good to see the sky again.

Jesse waited until Boone got off the ladder and they stood together on the rock shelf. The source of light came from around a rock outcropping. Jesse couldn't see beyond the obstruction.

"Think this is a trap?" Boone asked.

"Pretty sure it is," Jesse replied.

"You ready, then?"

Jesse gripped the handle of the strange gun. "Ready."

Together, they walked around the rock and into the light.

Chapter 21
The Wrong End of a Horse

The click of a gun being cocked echoed off the rock walls.

"Drop it," said a deep voice, full of gravel.

Boone stiffened. He recognized the voice, and the faint scents his human nose could pick out. If he'd been in dragon form, he would have caught those scents much sooner.

Squinting into the light of a rising sun, Boone realized they were at the back of a small cliff dwelling roughly fifty paces deep. It had fallen into disrepair and ruin, the adobe blocks that once framed it now tumbled to the sandy floor. Dragon glyphs decorated the walls of the cave, many of the same symbols that were on the map. Early morning light streamed in from a semi-circular opening on the far end of the cave through plant roots and vines that dangled over the edge. Against the light stood a man in a long leather coat, holding a six-shooter aimed at them.

Boone's face split into a grin. "Colorow!" he said.

Colorow didn't return the smile. "Drop it," he repeated, waving his gun in Jesse's direction.

Boone took a step forward. "I been worried sick," he said, "Where've you been all this—"

Colorow's pistol turned to Boone. "Not another step," he said sharply.

Boone froze, uncertain.

Jesse slowly pulled a strange contraption from under his belt and laid it on the ground. It looked like a gun, but no gun Boone had ever seen before. It was all copper wheels and cogs with a thick little barrel and a handle shaped like a bird. He wondered where Jesse had found the thing.

Colorow's face was in shadow, where he stood framed by the rising sun peeking over the mountains across the valley. Boone wished he could read Colorow's expression, not that the man ever gave anything away on his poker face.

"How did you get here?" Colorow asked. "I made sure the chimney was sealed from the tunnels below."

"The tommyknocker," Jesse said.

Colorow grunted. "I might have known," he said under his breath.

"Where's Eliza?" Jesse asked. There was a distant rumble of thunder.

"Fetching something for me. I planned to collect you two later."

"Sorry to ruin your plans," Boone said softly. He could feel anger growing in him—anger, hurt, and betrayal all mixed into a hard knot in the pit of his stomach.

"It doesn't matter. This works just as well."

"Collect us for what?" Jesse asked.

Colorow shifted his feet in the sand without moving the gun. "I thought you kids had figured out the map."

"We did," Jesse said.

"Then you'll know how important you three are."

Jesse and Boone gave each other puzzled frowns.

Colorow took a deep breath. "Boone, your reading skills are pathetic."

Boone's anger took a leap higher in his stomach.

"I really thought Frances' son would be smarter than this," Colorow continued, a sneer apparent in his voice.

Boone felt a growl growing in his throat. Frances was his mother, the dragon in cahoots with Orendos who had enslaved the Katsina in the Wité Pot before it was shattered.

"The three glyphs in the lower right corner of the map?" Colorow prompted in what was anything but a patient tone.

Boone looked around at the walls of the cliff dwelling. He noticed a familiar symbol etched into the stone to the right, half obscured by rubble. It was one of the people from the map, the one with horns, and suddenly he knew.

"The dragon," he said. "The glyph on the far right was the dragon."

Colorow grunted. "At least you learned something when you were with me."

Jesse nodded toward a symbol to the left of the cave, carved into the stone wall directly above what looked like the remains of a kiva. It was the person holding what Boone now realized looked like a plant.

"That's a..." Jesse seemed to be searching for the right word, "a terramage, isn't it?"

"And the last figure in the middle?" Colorow said.

"Orendos," Boone said quickly. They'd figured out that much.

But Colorow shook his head. "Not when it has a head. Didn't anyone ever tell you what kind of mage Orendos was?"

Boone was getting tired of the condescending note in Colorow's voice. He wondered why he'd never noticed it before. "No."

Jesse turned his head, looking back the way they'd come. The color drained from his face, and he said in a small voice, "A thundermage. Orendos was a thundermage."

Jesse stared at the figure carved in the rock directly behind them, right over the hidden entrance they'd come through. It was the person from the map, the one they'd assumed was this Orendos Boone talked about. The left hand held a circle with curved lines coming out of it and twisting together on top. The person's right arm was stretched straight out and had lines falling off it, lines that could be rain or snow or hail. Jesse felt a rush of cold wash through him, leaving him shivering.

"A thundermage is very rare indeed," Colorow said. "You are only the second mage to hold that incredible power. It is the power over life and death."

"What do you mean?" Jesse whispered.

"A raging storm overpowers anyone unlucky enough to be caught in it. On the other hand, a drought kills all life. Orendos knew that. More than two hundred years ago, there was an extreme drought in the west. The Katsina begged Orendos to end it. He obliged. It wasn't his fault the Katsina didn't like the price tag, but they could not avoid payment. Orendos had the entire Katsina council at his beck and call until Frances betrayed him." Jesse noticed Boone start back in apparent surprise. "Now *that* is power," Colorow continued. "Wouldn't you like to have such power, boy?"

"No," Jesse's mouth formed the word, but no sound came out.

"It is your destiny. That is why I planned to take you with me. When Boone reconstructs the Wité Pot, you will yield it. You will be the most powerful mage since Orendos."

To the left, near the symbol Jesse now knew was the terramage, a person emerged through the wall, walking out of it as if the rock were no more than a curtain to be pushed aside. It was Eliza.

Her face and arms were smudged with dirt, tear tracks still visible in the black on her cheeks. She carried a piece of fired clay in one hand. As she emerged, her eyes took in the scene, widening when they saw Boone and Jesse.

"What took you so long?" Colorow snapped as he turned to her, moving the gun in her direction.

In that moment, Boone moved. He leaped forward, shifting midair into dragon form with a roar that shook the cavern. Colorow brought his gun back around in a flash. He fired, hitting Boone somewhere in the shoulder, throwing him off balance and sending him crashing into the right wall of the cave.

Anger flooded Colorow's voice. "I wish I could finish you off right here and now."

A sound caught Jesse's ear and he looked down to see a glass marble roll past his feet and into the center of the room. Colorow turned away from Boone to stare at the marble.

"What—" he began.

"Duck!" Jesse heard someone whisper behind him.

Without stopping to think, Jesse dropped to the ground as several shots whizzed past above his head. Colorow looked up in surprise and suddenly melted before their eyes, morphing into some sort of misty vapor, like smoke. The shots cut through the vapor, separating it, but not hitting anything solid.

Jesse heard a curse and looked back in surprise to see Miss Dalton step out of the hidden entrance, sighting along the barrel of a rifle. Before Jesse had time to be shocked at his teacher's presence or the unladylike word coming from her mouth, he heard Eliza scream. He looked back to find her surrounded by the vapor.

Forgetting Miss Dalton's admonition to stay low, Jesse grabbed the odd gun he had taken from the treasure room and leaped to his feet, running toward Eliza.

"Jesse!" she screamed, reaching out a hand to him.

He tried to grab it, but she was turning to vapor too.

"Drop the shard," Miss Dalton yelled. "That's what he wants!"

Eliza was fading fast, the rock wall behind her and the petroglyph of a terramage visible through the wisp of her face. Her eyes flicked up to Miss Dalton, and Jesse saw Eliza's hand release the piece of clay pot she held.

With a gasp, she snapped back into solid form, falling to her knees as the vapor disappeared. Jesse dropped the gun and ran to prop her up.

Miss Dalton walked further into the chamber, slowly scanning it from side to side with her rifle at the ready.

"This just ain't my day," Boone groaned from the right side of the cavern. He scrabbled weakly at the rock wall with his claws, trying to stand. "That pistol must have been dragon-made."

"No doubt about it," Miss Dalton said as she reached the spot where Colorow had stood and knelt swiftly to retrieve her marble. "Your mother probably made that pistol." Boone looked askance at Miss Dalton. She didn't seem to notice. She examined the marble between her thumb and forefinger. "Good. It's not scratched. This is my last one."

"Seems like you ain't got no marbles left, firing at a skinwalker that way," Boone grumbled.

Turning to smile at Boone, Miss Dalton pocketed the marble and walked to his side, placing a hand near the rip in his scales that trickled a thin line of yellow blood.

"The gun was supposed to be a distraction while I trapped him in the marble, but he was too fast for me."

She traced a glyph over the wound, and Jesse watched with increasing shock as the wound closed and the scale became whole once again.

Eliza tried to stand up, but stumbled. She pushed away Jesse's hand when he reached out to support her. "He kidnapped my papa," Eliza said. She swayed unsteadily on her feet despite the steel in her voice.

Miss Dalton brushed off Boone's scale with a free hand and swung the rifle into a harness at her hip. "I'm well aware of that, Miss Matthews. I've been searching for your father for nearly five months."

"He said Papa would die if I didn't do what he asked."

Jesse saw a softness enter Miss Dalton's expression. "Don't worry, Eliza. Gloopna knows where he is. He'll soon be free."

"Gloopna?" Jesse asked.

"The tommyknocker."

"What, that little beggar?" Boone asked incredulously. He climbed to all fours and shook himself.

"The skinwalker had Gloopna enthralled. He was forced to kidnap Eliza's father and guard the treasure chamber by posing as a threatening Katsina. But I was able to break the enchantment." Miss Dalton grimaced. "That's why it took me so long to get up here."

Eliza crossed her arms over her chest. "That man, that *skinwalker*, still has the Wité Pot shard," she said.

"He won't leave this valley without you three. He needs you all to reassemble the pot." She looked down her nose at Jesse. "Especially you, Mr. Owens."

Jesse wanted to shake himself all over, as Boone had done. He climbed unsteadily to his feet. "Why me?" he asked.

"Only a thundermage can use the pot," she said. "That's how Frances set it up."

"My mother," Boone said.

Miss Dalton turned back to him. "Yes."

Boone spoke hesitantly. "Colorow, or whoever he really is, said Frances betrayed Orendos. What did he mean?"

Miss Dalton studied Boone for several long moments before speaking. "I don't know what the Katsina have told you about your mother and the war with Orendos."

"Aren't you a Katsina?" Jesse blurted. When she had healed Boone, Jesse thought for sure she must be one of the ruling council that his friends spoke of.

Miss Dalton chuckled. "Me? No. I'm a mirrormage. I hunt skinwalkers and trap them in a mirrored surface, like the marble, so they become harmless."

"I always thought my mother was in cahoots with Orendos," Boone said.

"She was," Miss Dalton replied. "Many years ago, there was a great drought in the land. The Katsina watched their people dying, and they could not stop it."

"I thought the Katsina were all powerful," Jesse said. "Why couldn't they do anything?"

"The Katsina are mages," Miss Dalton said, walking over to place a hand on Jesse's shoulder. "They each have a different type of power, just like me, just like you and Eliza. But they've been around for a while longer."

"Try a couple thousand years," Boone said.

"How do they live so long?" Jesse asked.

"Magic, if you want to call it that," Miss Dalton said. "It gives us unnaturally long life, in addition to our special powers."

"So, each mage can only do certain things with their power?" Jesse asked. He finally felt like he was starting to understand this crazy world of magic he'd involuntarily entered.

"Yes," Miss Dalton replied. "And controlling the weather is a very rare gift. There was only one person who held that power all those years ago."

"Orendos," Eliza said.

"The Katsina asked him to come here, to end the drought and bring life back to the land. He came, but he tricked them. A young dragonmage named Frances built Orendos a pot, the Wité Pot, that could trap the power and souls of other mages and bend them to his will. I don't think Frances fully realized what she had done when she followed the directions Orendos gave her. When she did, she could not back out, especially when Orendos threatened her son."

"And so she did his bidding," Boone said quietly.

"For a while. Orendos had other servants—we call them skinwalkers. They have existed since before the dawn of time, using an evil magic that is raw and untamed. Orendos taught them how to take on the shape of people by using a token stolen from the person they imitated. Skinwalkers were Orendos' spies. But he did not understand the power he tried to harness.

"Frances realized that the skinwalkers intended to take the power of the Wité Pot for themselves. If that happened, they would destroy the world. She could no longer turn a blind eye to what was happening. She protected her son as best she could and then she broke the pot, destroying Orendos and wounding herself. With the last of her strength, she hid the shards, using enchantment. To ensure the pot cannot be used without a balance of power, a different type of mage is required to retrieve each pot shard. Only a dragonmage can reforge it, and only a thundermage can wield it, because that is who Frances made it for in the first place. Just before she disappeared, Frances charged the newly freed Katsina with protecting the pot shards and raising her son."

"Where did she go?" Boone asked.

"No one knows, but her wound was serious. I'm sorry, but it's doubtful she survived."

Eliza put a hand on her hip and squinted at Miss Dalton. "My papa never told the story like that. He said the Katsina destroyed Orendos and broke the Wité Pot."

"That's what I was told," Boone said. "Begging your pardon, ma'am, but how do you know all this?"

Miss Dalton's lips curved up as she studied Boone. "Because I was the one who protected you and delivered you to the Katsina when Frances' work was done."

Jesse gave a start. Boone had said the war with this Orendos fellow was two hundred years ago. Was Miss Dalton really that old? To be told a mage had a long life was one thing. To have a woman standing in front of him who claimed to be two hundred years old was something else entirely. Pa would be surprised, to say the least.

Miss Dalton laughed, looking around at them each in turn. "Don't look so shocked! I was very young then, not much older than you three, and Frances was my friend. She saved me when I..." She faltered, catching Jesse's eye with a smile that had a hint of bitterness to it. "When I came into my power."

Boone smiled, his tongue lolling out the side of his jaws like a happy puppy's. "I think I remember you!" he said. "I knew I liked the scent of roses for a reason. You kept me hidden, didn't you, until you took me to the Katsina?"

Miss Dalton's smile faded. "It's time to hide you again." She pointed at the gun Jesse still held. "Where did you get that old thing?"

Jesse felt heat fill his cheeks. "Below. In that treasure room."

"I think it dates back to the time before Orendos. It probably has some strong magic, if it still works. Maybe you'd do well to hang on to it for a while."

Jesse nodded and tucked it back under his belt.

"That skinwalker is a wily one," Miss Dalton continued. "It took me awhile to realize that he wasn't the real Colorow. When I did, he disappeared in that cave in he forced Gloopna to create in the Ulay. He's tipped his hand now, and he's after you three to help him remake the Wité Pot."

Eliza hung her head. "He already got my cooperation," she mumbled.

Miss Dalton moved her hand to Eliza's shoulder. "Even before the Wité Pot was made, Orendos was very good at taking hostages to force people to do his bidding. The skinwalkers learned a lot from Orendos."

"Hostages?" Jesse asked. An alarming thought occurred to him.

Miss Dalton looked sharply at Jesse. He could see the same thought come into her mind as the blood drained out of her face. "Where did you last see your father?" she asked.

Chapter 22
Die Standin' Up

Jesse was the last to climb onto Boone's back just before the dragon launched himself out of the cliff dwelling. For a split second, Jesse thought the combined weight of three people was too much for Boone and they would drop like a stone into the lake below. But then, Boone's wings caught the wind and they glided down to the clearing where Jesse had last seen Pa.

A mist rose from the lake in the early morning light, giving the scene an eerie, otherworldly feel. Sagging, broken trees with limbs scarred black from lightning drooped toward the ground, as if dying. Only the water of the lake still looked as untouched and pristine as ever beneath the mist, reflecting the morning sun and the clouds beginning to gather overhead.

Jesse slid off Boone's back and ran to the rock where Pa had taken shelter from the storm. There was no one there.

"The whole town was probably out looking for you after the storm," Eliza said as she slid off Boone's back. "Your pa could be anywhere by now."

"Step aside," Boone said, coming up behind them.

Jesse stumbled back as Boone's huge dragon head slid forward, pressing into the crevice under the rock. His forked tongue flicked out between sharp teeth. "New-turned earth and molasses," Boone said. "That's what your pa smells like."

"You smell with your tongue?" Eliza asked. "That is disgusting."

"What?" Boone protested. "You don't think smelling through a *nose* is disgusting? The sharpest scents fall on the tongue."

Eliza rolled her eyes.

Boone lifted his head, swiveling it back and forth while his tongue flicked in and out between his teeth. He tromped around the clearing and to the lake's edge, then out into the trees. Every few steps, he would pause and test the air with his tongue before resuming his exploration. Finally, he returned.

"I think your pa left and came back here," Boone said. "There's a stronger scent over there by that fallen tree."

"That's the tree that fell when I was trying to catch Rio," Jesse said.

"He was probably trying to pick up on your trail. But the freshest scents are over there, by the edge. I can smell Colorow there too."

Jesse swallowed hard. "You don't think Pa—"

"No!" Eliza said quickly. "The skinwalker needs your papa alive, or he won't be able to force you to use the pot."

"Not *in* the lake," Boone said, swinging his great scaled muzzle. "Across it. My best guess is that Colorow took your pa to that island in the middle. C'mon. I can fly you over there."

"No!" Miss Dalton strode in front of them, standing between Boone and the lake. "You're not running off to fight a skinwalker, Boone Evans," she said firmly. "Nor are any of you. Frances would never forgive me if her son reforged the Wité Pot and was enslaved to it like she was enslaved."

"What about my pa?" Jesse asked.

"I've been hunting skinwalkers for two hundred years, Jesse. I think I can handle this one." She dug the marble out of her pocket and slid the rifle from its holster. "The best thing for you kids to do is take cover. Stay hidden, and stay safe."

"Not an option, Delilah," a voice said behind her.

Some of the mist over the lake came together, gathering rapidly to become Colorow striding out of the water. Miss

Dalton spun, bringing her rifle to her shoulder, but she wasn't fast enough. He already had his pistol aimed directly at her.

"I wouldn't do that if I were you," he said calmly.

Miss Dalton scowled at him a moment before throwing her rifle to the ground, where it landed in the mud at the edge of the lake.

Jesse's fingers itched to pull the gun from beneath his belt. He could hardly keep from running at Colorow and slugging him. Thunder rumbled in the distance, and for once Jesse didn't care that his anger was bringing on a storm. "What have you done with my pa?" he asked in a low, menacing voice.

Colorow's lips twitched in what might have been a smile. "He's quite safe. You just come along with me quietly, and everything will be fine. As soon as we find the last two shards of the Wité Pot, your dragon friend will reforge it. With that pot, you will rule the west, maybe even the world. You can allow your father to rule by your side, if you like."

"My pa would never want that. Not for me, not for himself," Jesse said between gritted teeth.

Out of the corner of his eye, Jesse saw Eliza kneel swiftly on the ground, plunging her hands into the soil. There was a rumbling sound, as if the earth complained at being disturbed, and a ripple went through the ground, rushing forward to hit the lake where Colorow still stood. He wavered, narrowly catching his balance. Swinging his arm around, he fired the pistol at Eliza.

"Eliza, no!" Jesse yelled.

She dodged to the side, but the bullet hit her and sent her falling back onto the ground with a cry.

In that moment, Miss Dalton threw her marble as hard as she could at Colorow. At the same time, she traced a symbol in the air, a circle with curved lines twisted together at the top that glowed a bright red before she pushed it. Like a hot branding iron, it rushed at Colorow, following the arc of the marble she had thrown.

He was fast. He caught the marble in his free hand. The glyph was only moments behind it. Colorow's eyes widened as he saw it coming, and suddenly he was no longer there. The marble fell into the lake with a sinking plunk. Miss Dalton cursed in a very unladylike fashion and fished her rifle out of the mud.

"Get out of here," she yelled at Boone. "Take Eliza and Jesse and fly!"

Boone didn't need to be told twice. He leaped over her, landing with a crash beside Jesse and crouching so Jesse could clamber on.

"Eliza is hurt," Jesse said.

"I can carry her," Boone replied.

Jesse gripped a tuft of fur at the base of Boone's neck and scrambled over the slippery scales until he could swing one leg around and find a secure perch just in front of the wing joints. Picking up Eliza gently in one giant claw, Boone sprang into the air with his back legs.

As they climbed into the sky, Jesse realized it was clouding over more quickly now. Like dust kicked up by a stampeding herd of buffalo, dark clouds that roiled and flashed lightning mushroomed in from all sides, blotting out the sun. Yet again, he had called up a storm he couldn't control. At least he could do something to help Miss Dalton.

"Put Eliza on that island," Jesse yelled at Boone. "She should be safe there for a little while."

"But Miss Dalton said—"

"We're going back," Jesse said, yanking out the strange gun. "I ain't done with that fancy-pants skinwalker."

Boone grunted. "Now that's what I like to hear!"

Gliding down to the island in the middle of the lake, Boone landed on his back legs and gently placed Eliza on the ground. Her skin was a pasty color, her expression pinched with pain. She cradled one arm in the other. Blood stained the sleeve of her dress around a tear where the bullet appeared to have grazed her on the right shoulder.

"What do you two think you're doing?" Eliza would have snapped at them fiercely with one hand on her hip, Jesse knew, if she hadn't been fighting the pain of the bullet wound.

"Helping Miss Dalton," Jesse said with a huff.

"She said she didn't need help."

The sound of a gun firing drifted to them from across the water. Jesse whipped around, looking back the way they'd come, only to see Miss Dalton fall backwards, landing in the mud at the water's edge. Colorow was standing over her menacingly.

"C'mon, Boone!" Jesse urged.

Jesse felt more than heard a rumble begin in Boone's throat. "Hang on!" the dragon yelled.

Boone took to the air again. Jesse grabbed fistfuls of fur and tightened his knees as Boone climbed. In moments, Eliza was no more than a speck, the lake a puddle. They flew up into the clouds, and Jesse began to fear they would get hit by a lightning bolt.

Angling back down, Boone tucked his wings in, falling faster and faster. The wind whipped past, tugging harder and harder at Jesse. He held on for all he was worth, terrified of what would happen if he slipped off the dragon's back.

As they got closer, the rumbling Jesse felt from inside the dragon got stronger. Colorow looked up. At this distance, it was impossible to read his expression, even if he gave away more than a twitch of the lips. He must have been frightened, because he began to run.

Jesse whooped in triumph as Boone opened his mouth and fire gushed out. It followed Colorow as he raced for the trees, hitting several of those still damaged by the earlier storm. They burst into flames, and soon the blaze raced from treetop to treetop around the clearing.

The trees were coming up fast, and Jesse was afraid they would crash into them. But Boone spread his wings and angled his body away so they swooped upward. They cleared the trees by no more than a foot. As Boone went past, Colorow leaped out of the trees and grabbed on to Boone's tail. They climbed into the air with Colorow still hanging on.

Boone shook his tail back and forth. "Get off!"

The movement made them jerk to the side and back again. It was all Jesse could do to hang on.

Colorow had no such difficulty. He clung to the dragon like a wicked spider and pulled himself up the tail until he reached Boone's back.

Jesse tried to bring his own gun around to fire at Colorow, but Boone's motion prevented Jesse from aiming.

Then it started to rain. Boone's scales became slicker, and Jesse needed both hands wrapped firmly in the fur to keep his seat.

If only Jesse could force the storm to do his bidding and call a lightning bolt to strike Colorow down! Closing his eyes, Jesse concentrated. He searched for that inner heat he had noticed when he somehow created the lightning ball in the basilisk cave. *Please, please.* He willed himself to find a way, wanting to control the magic so much that he ached inside. *Please!* He imagined what he wanted to happen, a lightning bolt flashing out of the sky and hitting Colorow. He pictured it and wished for it with everything he had. When he opened his eyes, the clouds above swirled just as they had before. The lightning flashed in random patterns, with no acknowledgement of the world below. It was a storm like any other. He could not control it. He could not change it. He felt a sinking despair.

Colorow stood slowly and advanced along Boone's spine, holding the pistol. His face had more expression than Jesse had ever seen on it. It was full of anger and hatred. "I wanted to use Frances' son to remake the pot," Colorow shouted. "But you are not the only dragonmage in the world!"

Jesse ducked, but Colorow was not aiming for him. The pistol fired, the bullet whizzing past Jesse's ear and leaving it ringing as it hit Boone's neck. With a roar that ended in a gurgle, Boone shuddered. Then he was fighting to stay aloft.

At the same moment, Colorow made a flying leap and tackled Jesse. The momentum carried them both off Boone's back and into the air. Lightning flashed all around them, and Jesse was sure he was about to die.

But then the world grew misty, and he realized that he could see the clouds through Colorow's skin. His ears popped, making the thunder seem louder than before, and suddenly, he was falling onto the bank beside Miss Dalton.

Colorow bent to retrieve Miss Dalton's rifle and clean the mud from it. The snap of a twig from the depths of the trees across the clearing brought Colorow's head up. He stepped toward the sound suspiciously.

Jesse shook his teacher. "Miss Dalton!" he hissed. "Stop him! He's trying to take me away!"

Miss Dalton groaned, her eyelids fluttering. "My last marble," she whispered. "It's gone."

"Don't you have anything else that will work?"

"I'm a mirrormage," Miss Dalton said. She swallowed hard and opened her eyes. "I have to have a mirror."

Jesse's eyes caught the glint of lightning reflecting off the surface of the lake. "The lake is a mirror," he whispered.

Miss Dalton struggled to push herself up onto an elbow. "What?"

"The lake is a mirror," Jesse said more firmly. "Can you use it?"

Miss Dalton nodded and winced at the movement. "Distract him. Use your magic."

Panic jabbed Jesse's insides. "But I can't control—"

He couldn't say more before Colorow grabbed his arm and yanked him to his feet. "We're getting out of here now," he said.

"You'll wanna step away from my boy, Mister," said a voice from behind Colorow.

Jesse looked up to see Pa standing at the edge of the clearing, holding his Army-issue rifle. The treetops burned behind him, the fire radiating heat as it inched its way toward the ground and filled the air with smoke.

Pa looked tattered and worn. His clothes and skin were streaked with black, his face gaunt with a haunted look in his eyes that Jesse had never seen before. It scared him.

"Finally," Colorow said. "I've found your father."

Jesse realized that Colorow had never held Pa hostage, but had allowed Jesse to think he did. He fumbled at his belt for the strange gun.

"What is that?" Colorow sneered. "Some child's toy?"

Jesse tried to yank the gun free, but one of the coils caught and the gun slipped from his fingers, falling to the ground with a clatter.

"We're leaving now," said Colorow.

The clearing became hazy, as if it was unraveling before his very eyes.

"No! Pa!" he screamed.

Pa fired his rifle. Colorow was hit before he could do anything about it. Frowning, Colorow looked down at the wound in his chest. Jesse waited for him to fall, but he didn't. The hole closed over, and Colorow laughed. Pa took a step back, his expression full of fear and loathing.

Then Colorow swung his hands out, and they transformed into flowing lines of smoke that flew at Pa, pushing him back into the burning trees.

Jesse stared at the spot where Pa had stood. He felt hollow inside. Pa was gone too, just like Ma. Jesse didn't know if he could stand the agony that suddenly hit him in the gut. He doubled over and noticed the odd gun in the mud at his feet. Reaching down slowly, he picked it up. The diamond eye on the bird handle began to glow red.

The clearing came into sharp focus around Jesse as he stood back up. It seemed as though he could see each glowing ember, burning needle, and blade of grass. The heat from the fire grew more intense, as if he were the one who had fallen into the flames, not Pa.

Colorow grabbed at Jesse's arm again, then yelped and let go, stepping back to stare at Jesse with wide eyes. Jesse was dimly aware of the storm above, swirling faster and responding to his thoughts.

Trees broke free of the ground, swirling up into the vortex building in the clouds above. Flashes of lightning hit the ground and set more trees on fire.

But none of the lightning broke the surface of the water. The raging wind bent trees all around the lake without touching the water itself. It remained calm and still, reflecting the storm all around it like a mirror.

"Whatever you're doing," Colorow yelled against the wind, "stop! It will only hurt you and the ones you love."

Jesse took careful aim at the pot shard Colorow still held in one hand. "If I destroy the shard," he said calmly, "you'll have no reason to threaten them again."

Colorow smiled and disappeared in the smoke of the clearing.

Jesse squeezed the trigger.

The gun clicked and whirled and began to whine. Jesse wanted to cover his ears, but he held the gun steady, aimed at where the pot shard had been. There a popping sound, like a cork escaping a bottle, and suddenly Colorow was standing in the clearing again, mouth hanging open in shock. As Jesse watched, Colorow was enveloped in coppery flames that died down almost as quickly as they began. Instead of the man Jesse had known as Colorow, an oily black shadow hovered over the clearing. It had sickly orange and green patches that glistened wetly.

An unearthly howl came from the figure as it raced toward the lake, right into Miss Dalton's red glyph where it hovered in the air over the water.

Throwing its arms out, the shadow screamed in anger as its body was sucked down into the surface of the lake until the scream broke off abruptly and the black shadow was covered in water. Rainbows flashed under the surface, as if the lake contained colored lightning, before the surface became still once again.

Jesse heard the whinny of a horse and turned to see Rio come galloping out of the trees from the direction of the mine.

"Boone!" Miss Dalton tried to get to her feet, but stumbled and fell back in the mud.

Jesse looked across the lake to where Miss Dalton pointed. The huge red dragon plummeted out of the sky and plowed into a stand of trees on the island.

Jesse's jaw firmed with determination. He gave a sharp whistle. "Rio!"

Boone fell out of the sky and toward the island. A buzzing sound filled his ears and he wanted to swat away the swarm of flies that filled his head, but he couldn't move.

He came down through a stand of trees, breaking off limbs and trunks that tried to spear him on his way through until he hit the ground with a heavy thud that shook the small island. He coughed, trying to breathe air that felt thick and heavy.

He was dimly aware of Eliza running up to him at a jagged pace and placing her free hand on his muzzle.

"Boone!" Her voice was a faint echo from somewhere far away. "Hang on!"

She closed her eyes and began to tremble, but he felt only a wisp of warmth inside that soon faded.

Eliza opened her eyes as tears slid down her cheeks. "It will be okay," she said in a choked voice that clearly meant it wouldn't.

Boone fought the panic that rose within him. He tried to get up, but it only made him cough more.

Boone knew he was dying when he noticed a figure riding toward him across the water on a horse. It looked like Jesse, but he was different. His hair crackled with streaks of lightning. His skin glowed brighter than the flames raging in the trees on the bank behind him. His eyes were swimming pools of molten alloy, flashing and snapping.

The horse he rode resembled Rio, but its chestnut fur had turned to transparent glass that revealed white clouds roiling inside. Ice flew from its hooves, and the lake froze in its wake as it galloped directly toward Boone.

The transformed Jesse pulled up his horse sharply behind Eliza and slid off the mount as smooth as melting butter. Eliza stared at him.

"Help me," Jesse said to her with a voice like the roar of a furnace.

Jesse and Eliza each grabbed a giant claw, and Boone jerked as an electric current went through his body. His back arced. His limbs jerked beyond his control, beating against the ground like an Indian's drum.

Boone's scream came out high and thin at first. It rose to a wail, growing louder, expanding, deepening as he felt the fire focus on his throat, expand, and fill it.

With a roar that shook the ground, Boone burst into the air. He beat his wings once, then twice. He stretched his neck. He could breathe again.

Looking down, he saw Jesse and Eliza grinning up at him. Jesse looked normal now, holding Rio's reins and rubbing an arm that no longer looked like it was on fire. Boone wondered if it had all been part of a fevered dream. He glided back down to the ground and landed in front of them.

"What happened?" he gasped.

Eliza perched one hand on her hip in spite of the grin on her face. "A polite 'thank you' would be in order, I should think."

Jesse peered at Boone, a frown pulling down the edges of his mouth. Boone began to wonder if they'd put him back together in the wrong order.

"Boone," Jesse finally said. "Where's your hat?"

Chapter 23
Leaking Out of the Landscape

B oone studied the hats perched neatly in a row on the shelf, trying to ignore the smell of ice cream wafting from the soda counter on the other side of the store. He had been without a hat for just over a week. His nose was sunburned.

"Well?" Miss Dalton asked. "Are you going to take all day?"

Boone picked up the sienna hat on the right and placed it on his head. "Too tight," he said with a frown as he put it back on the shelf. He missed his old hat. It was a custom job, and no dry goods store variety could replace it.

Miss Dalton gave an impatient sigh. "We're late, Boone," she said, looking down at the watch pinned to her bodice.

Boone grabbed a hat from the middle of the rack. "Let's go," he said, striding to the cash register.

While George rang up his purchase, Boone stared longingly at a kid sitting at the soda counter, savoring the last bites of a vanilla sundae.

"You sure I can't tempt you with one last scoop before you hit the road?" George asked with a smile.

From the corner of his eye, Boone saw Miss Dalton frown. The woman was worse than Colorow when it came to sweets. He sighed. "Naw. Best be on my way."

"Good journey to you, then," George said.

Boone tipped the new hat onto his head before following Miss Dalton out of the store. "That remains to be seen," he mumbled.

Jesse sat on the knoll at his favorite fishing spot, staring out across the calm water of the lake as it caught the sunlight and a fish leaped from the depths after a horsefly. A burnt smell lingered in the air and many of the trees were broken and battered, reminding him of the destruction he had recently caused. It was just as well that he would soon be gone from this beautiful place.

In his hands, he turned over and over the bottle he had carried around in his pocket for the last several days. The glass caught the reflection of the sun, making the dirt inside seem to sparkle. He tried to conjure up Ma's smile as she brushed a lock of hair off his forehead or handed him a thick slice of hot bread dripping with butter, but he was starting to forget exactly what she looked like.

Pushing aside the wistful ache in his chest, Jesse slowly climbed to his feet. He pulled back one arm and threw the bottle as hard as he could. It sailed out over the lake, spinning in the sunshine and catching the light one last time as it arced down and hit the water with a small splash, sinking quickly out of sight.

Jesse was about to leave when his eye caught something on the shore where the water gently lapped at it. He came down off the knoll and approached the shore, breath quickening as he got closer. It was the Wité Pot shard. It hadn't been destroyed with Colorow after all. Jesse felt his fingers trembling as he bent to pick it up.

For the cause of so much trouble, the shard seemed pretty ordinary. Ridges skirted one side, while dark lines swirled and swept over the pale red clay in an incomplete pattern. If Jesse could destroy the shard, no one would ever be able to rebuild the Wité Pot or force him to use it.

He tried squeezing it, but that only gave him a sore palm. Crushing it with his boot heel on a rock didn't work, either. The shard was obviously not an ordinary piece of fired clay. He wondered if he should throw it back into the lake or bury it. Finally, he slipped the shard into his pocket. Maybe Miss Dalton would know how to get rid of the thing for good.

Jesse could see his family waiting for him in the yard as he approached the cabin. Pa's skin was red and raw from the fire, but he insisted he was as healthy as Rio, who stamped impatiently and jerked against the lead Pa held.

"Where've you been?" Mary scolded Jesse with a half smile. "The others will be here any minute."

"The boy had some thinking to do, Mary," Pa said. He handed Jesse the reins to Rio. "I don't understand all this hoity-toity magic business," Pa said quietly. "But I do know one thing. Last week, I thought I'd lost you for good, and it come near to ripping me right in two. I want you to take extra care of yourself in this canyon place. I don't reckon I'd be around much longer if I were to lose you and your ma both."

Jesse stared at the reins gripped tightly in his fists as a warm glow spread through him. He had felt the same when he watched Colorow push Pa into the flames. It had been a huge relief to find him alive and safe.

"I love you too, Pa," he mumbled.

Sam clapped Pa on the shoulder and stuck out a hand for Jesse to shake, pulling him into a bear hug. "Don't do no more growing while you're gone, Sprout," he said. "You're half again as tall as when you got here." He pounded Jesse on the back hard enough to make him cough.

"Sam!" Mary scolded. She handed Jesse a saddlebag. "I added an extra pair of socks and underwear."

Jesse blushed. "Thanks," he mumbled.

The heat in his face got hotter as Mary went up on tiptoe to kiss his cheek. "You take care, you hear?"

"I hope this fancy learning of Miss Dalton's won't turn you into some city dude," Sam said with a wink.

"Don't worry," Boone said as he came up behind them. "I'll keep him in line."

Jesse turned to see a funny little hat perched on Boone's head. It was a deep chocolate brown with a rounded top and a short brim. It made Boone's head look bigger, his ginger hair wilder as it flew up in a tangled cloud around the hat.

"What?" Boone said.

Jesse squelched a grin. "I ain't saying nothing."

Miss Dalton and the Matthews entered the yard behind Boone. Allan led a bay mare that Eliza rode side-saddle. Her Indian father, Mr. Matthews, leaned heavily on Allan's shoulder and his wife's arm. He wore a fancy suit with a top hat, but he was frail and gaunt from his imprisonment underground, his skin the color of stale paste with dark circles around his eyes.

"Are you sure you won't accompany us and visit the healers, Katsina Nukpana?" Miss Dalton asked Mr. Matthews.

He shook his head, a haunted smile extending fine wrinkles over his face. "Thank you, Delilah, but I only need rest and time."

"Do I have to leave you, Papa?" Eliza asked.

He reached up to pat one of her gloved hands. "Yes, my darling. It is time. The Katsina in the Veiled Canyon will teach you things I cannot."

"Don't worry, dear," Mrs. Matthews added. "Allan will be with you."

Jesse caught his breath as Allan gave him a triumphant smile.

"Does he have to come along?" Jesse whispered to Boone.

Boone shrugged. "A young lady like Eliza don't travel by herself."

"What are we, then—ghosts?"

Pa took the saddlebag from Jesse and threw it across Rio's back. "Mount up, son," he said. "I expect Miss Dalton is ready to be on her way."

Jesse tried to pretend he didn't see Miss Dalton step forward to place a hand gently on Pa's arm.

"I'll take good care of him, Paul," she said softly.

Pa covered her hand in his own. "I know you will."

Trying to hide his embarrassment, Jesse shoved a foot into the stirrup and swung onto Rio's back. "I hope you'll help me write to Pa," he said to Miss Dalton without looking directly at her.

She smiled up at him. "Every week."

"And I'll let you know how things are going on the home front, son," Pa added. He hesitated, looking at his hand still resting over Miss Dalton's. "If you like, Delilah, I could send a letter or two your way as well."

Now it was Miss Dalton's turn to blush. "That would be nice," she said quietly. She slowly pulled her hand away and opened her umbrella. "Come along, children. It's time to go or we'll miss the rendezvous." She led the way back up the road to the lake.

Jesse followed Eliza's horse. They both waved until the trees hid their families from view.

"Will I ever see them again?" Jesse asked quietly.

"Sure!" Boone said. He kept pace with Jesse, but stayed several steps away from Rio. "I'll fly you home anytime you ask."

"No, you won't," Miss Dalton called sternly over her shoulder.

Boone frowned at her back. "Humans never look up."

"It's not humans I'm worried about."

293

"How are we getting to the Veiled Canyon, then?" Jesse asked Boone. "You can't fly there, and winter's coming on. We'll never make it on horses."

Boone looked up at Jesse and winked. "Glyph circle."

"What's that?" Jesse was getting tired of Boone's peculiar jargon. "You draw a circle on the rock?"

"Sorta. You remember that cliff dwelling above the lake?"

"How can I forget it?" Jesse grumbled.

"Them glyphs drawn on the wall form a circle the Katsina can use to travel from one place to the next. Miss Dalton's arranged with the Katsina back home to meet us there and take us to the Veiled Canyon."

"So we're traveling by magic?"

Boone squirmed a little. "It ain't the most comfortable way to travel, but it does the job."

A familiar figure rounded the bend ahead, coming toward them leading a donkey that brayed loudly.

"Good day, folks." Mad Madge nodded politely to Miss Dalton, Eliza, and Allan. She stopped when she came to Boone and Jesse. "You boys find your fortune yet?" she asked with a toothless grin.

Jesse thought about the shard still in his pocket and the strange gun he'd buried in his saddlebag. "Yeah," he said. "I guess we did."

"Wish I could say the same. You know, I can't find hide nor hair of that treasure cave I showed you boys. It's like it up and walked away. I reckon it really was cursed."

"Maybe so." Boone's expression made it obvious he knew more than he was telling.

"So, ya'll are headed out of town, I see," Madge said, looking back at Miss Dalton and the Matthews. Miss Dalton had slowed and was impatiently waiting for them to catch up.

"Just for a little while," Jesse replied.

"Speaking of which," Boone said, tipping his new hat to Madge, "we'd best be on our way now."

Jesse pressed Rio's sides with his knees, and the horse followed Boone on up the road.

"Don't let the weeds grow around your ankles, I always say." Madge hitched her thumbs behind the straps of her overalls, giving them a friendly wave. "When you come back, old Madge will have a big pot of slumgullion on the boil for you."

Boone picked up his pace. "I don't know about you, kid, but that's all the encouragement I need to run for the hills!"

Acknowledgements

Special thanks go out to my cheerleading squad. This book wouldn't be possible without the unfailing support of my family and friends. Thank you for your enthusiasm.

I'm glad I had Julie Wright and Tristi Pinkston to clean up my messes. They did a fantastic job on the editing, as did my junior editors in Boone's Beta Club. You guys rock!

I had some amazing artists in my court. Michele Amatrula created an inspiring cover illustration, and Melissa Bigney put the finishing touches on it. I'm also indebted to the skills of Chad Griffiths for the book trailer animation.

I'm happy to have a family of bookworms with which to share my love of literature, and I'm grateful for the unfailing support of my husband. Without him, I would never have the strength or courage to reach for the stars.

Finally, I wish to thank my Heavenly Father for the talent, the inspiration, and the opportunity to pursue my dream.

 **Shauna E. Black** was born in Panama, but soon gave up jungle humidity for mountain air when her family moved to Utah. Since then, her head has always been in the clouds, and her nose in a book. She determined at a tender age that someday she would be a writer and still keeps years of scribbled, half-baked manuscripts in the attic.

Shauna lives in the Southwest with her husband and four children. She gleans inspiration from exploring the high desert and many Anasazi ruins near her home.

Made in the USA
San Bernardino, CA
23 February 2014